and *Mother to a Stranger*) and one short story collection (*Different Kinds of Love*). *Mother to a Stranger* (Blackstaff Press, 2002) has been published to critical acclaim in Germany. She has also published collections of poetry, stage plays and radio plays. Leland Bardwell currently lives in County Sligo.

The House

Leland Bardwell ,

BLACKSTAFF
PRESS
—
BELFAST

First published in 1984 by
Brandon Publishers Limited
Dingle, Co. Kerry

This edition published in 2006 by
Blackstaff Press
4c Heron Wharf, Sydenham Business Park
Belfast BT3 9LE
with the assistance of
the Arts Council of Northern Ireland

Typeset by CJWT Solutions, Newton-le-Willows, Merseyside
Printed in England by Cromwell Press
A CIP catalogue record for this book is available from the British Library
ISBN 0-85640-783-6

www.blackstaffpress.com

CHAPTER ONE

I REMEMBER ABOUT HALF A CENTURY ago walking up this staircase having had a row with my elder sister Maria. As a matter of fact I probably ran and I probably shouted: I hate you, I hate you.

What had she done to me? She had a scorching tongue, that's for certain. But in spite of the fact that my memory is usually very clear about childhood events – especially nasty ones – the details of this particular episode elude me.

However, as I sit here at the top of the stairs making maps out of paint scars – another childish preoccupation (every ceiling in the world seems to have had a map of Ireland on it) – I am thinking more of the present. Of my father with his old head mottled and coarse as a swede. Of Mother who had she married someone else might have been a slattern, even happy. But no. Mother could never forgive Father for being a Stewart, a mere member of the professional classes. Yes, believing herself to be of aristocratic lineage, Mother was a snob. Still is.

Now poor Father's wits are gone. There he was tonight at dinner whimpering for a glass of wine while Mother, stolid as a Carthaginian tomb carving, gazed at him with her basilisk eye.

And Theresa, of whom I have been conscious for fifty-three years, absent in the shadows of the dining room, her face blending with her white blouse, hard to catch in the candlelight, disturbing me more than anything else.

What an awful meal! Didn't I swear six years ago I'd never again sit at that table? After the row. But here I am back with my obsessions, my crackpot sentimentality for the place of my birth. Was it Uncle John Fitzgibbon or Uncle Mathew Barton who gave me my first sea-horse? Which led to what? Sea-mat, starfish, sponges, cowrie shells. To hear the sea when I was stuffed in my school uniform at Rugby. The names slide over my tongue.

Oh, Theresa! My hand is limp against the dark green paint of the stairwell. Down to the white rock with us to see the sea larking with its crusted waves. How it soaks our shoes and how the pebbles bruise our insteps.

Memories adorned with absence; better concentrate on the mean times. The lean times: me mooning around the garden against the crack of Richard's cricket bat; Ma's exalted cries of admiration as he hits a six into the fuchsia; me rigid, scholarly with dismissal of the physical activities of my younger brother just because I couldn't play the damned game as well as he.

But today – tonight, that is – Mother with her lies made me sick. 'If only you'd told me the exact date of your arrival.' Father, shaking over the cauliflower, the hand hovering and then falling right into the middle of his plate. My useless attempt to clean his fingers. Then after dinner it was worse. How I kept turning over the photographs on the mantelpiece: Richard, with bat and ball, squint-eyed in the sun – one I took with my Brownie box camera; Richard, profile, on a tall dock-tailed horse; Richard, scrubbed like he'd just come out of hospital, a little maneen in a suit, handkerchief peeping out of breast pocket and the dog, a photographer's prop, gazing at him with misty eyes.

'A photographer's prop,' I told Mother. Taken in Dawson Street, 1929.

'She said,' Mother sighed.

'Who?' I queried.

'The maid – oh I forget – the one we had when Uncle John died.'

'That was much later, Mother,' I said. 'I remember because he gave me a wind-up gramophone in 1934 after my second year at Rugby. We had recordings of Caruso and later Gigli and some early McCormacks as well.'

The gramophone shut like a suitcase and I used to carry it out into the garden, books of heavy records under my arm and those light tinny sounds would briefly fill the grass and gooseberry bushes ... *Che gelida manina* ... The rest of the family didn't like that kind of music so the shrubs and the shelter they gave from marauding ears were all the more essential. The little tins of needles with His Master's Voice, complete with dog and horn, were useful for trinkets later.

And then I made an awful mistake. This evening, I mean. I picked up a photograph of Maria and Father saw me. He had been put at the window and was clutching the curtain as though it were a soother when something or some old spiral of memory woke him up. He darted forward and began to claw my face.

'I took this,' I said, trying to calm him.

But 'girlie ... girlie ... ' ran out of his mouth with spittle.

'Here ... you hold it, Father.' I had to push him into the chair. In that neutered state I felt as though I'd just got up from a long illness. My legs shook as I ran from the room and tumbled up these stairs.

Where I sit now. Doing what? Trying to retrain myself to be tough, manly, self-assured. Me, a rich and successful historian with a flat full of valuable artefacts stolen from the four corners of the world. Trying to be decisive about my next move.

If only Theresa were here sitting beside me then my mind might get on with its manly business but I keep seeing the chimneypiece with the row of photographs in their silver frames: Jess and Maria on the swing, me in shorts, hair plastered down, with a book – God ... typical! – on my knee.

And not a single snap of brother James. James, the black sheep who escaped to be happy and has, it appears, ended up broke with an unfaithful wife and two delinquent daughters. Yes, ran away he did, brave lovely leonine James, all the way to Mauritius. Took ship to settle on the far side of the world, to marry a dark lady and make me thick with envy. So Ma and Pa took his photo away and wiped him off the slate. Until six years ago. All that partly the cause of the row, the one that made me swear I'd never return but let them stew, and I didn't – the proof being my overweight body trembling at the top of the stairs at this moment unrepentant of my weakness. Yes, something has to be settled once and for all.

My childhood is like a sheet all round me, like the closed doors on the landing behind me, the empty children's rooms; Theresa downstairs, cleaning up the debris of the meal; Ma toasting her hands this way and that in front of the fire; Pa monosyllabic, limp as old clothes, hunched in his chair.

CHAPTER TWO

WHAT YEAR DID I LEAVE SCHOOL – '34? '35? Let's see. Maria (the eldest) left Cheltenham College the year before the Spanish Civil War broke out. So it must have been two years before that that Cedric – he could even be called handsome – is running down these stairs. Yes, it's sunny and Jess is sitting on the garden seat facing the copper beech. In the dapple of leaves her face has the colour and texture of seedcake. She is reading, heavily wrapped in rugs in spite of the beautiful weather.

'Ah, Bunyan,' Cedric says. 'How learned. Thank heaven I don't have to go back to school. "His vassals, also to show their wills and supposed but ignoble gallantry, exercise themselves in their arms every day, and teach one another feats of war; they also defied their enemies, and sang up their praises of their tyrant … " Speaking of which, what time does Pa get home tonight?'

Jess squints up at him. She has a lot of annoying habits, the worst being a tendency to sniff between every sentence. A not-friendly-but-rather-disapproving sniff at that.

'The usual,' she says, or sniffs, 'you've only been away three months.'

'The summer term is the worst, as long as hell, or as Oxford Street.' He's rather proud that he knows England better than the others do.

But to go back to this evening. After the meal ended and

the old people had hobbled out I went over to Theresa.

'She's indefatigable. She knew damn well I was coming.'

'She had to play her little game.' Theresa begins to wipe the table with energy beyond her years.

'And she's decided to kill him. Inch by inch. How long has he been like this?'

'He's failed badly these last few months.'

'Hiding.'

'Yes. He's tired. She is too.'

'Oh Theresa, you are loyal. You know she'll die sitting up with her hand on her fork.'

'Don't be too hard on her.'

We look into each other's eyes and she says, 'Come.'

At the window a heavy wind sweeps in as she throws open the casement and at last I smell the eucalyptus.

'That's what I smell in London, mostly, before falling asleep.'

'There are seeds, now,' Theresa says. 'You can buy them in these new foreign shops. Indian seeds. They smell the same. Elachi, they're called. It's a jungle since Mr Barton died,' she adds.

'It's better like this. The palm tree keeps watch with its semaphore leaves.'

'Sentry go, you used to say.'

'How long has he, do you think?'

'He could go any day.'

'I wonder what he thinks about. Does he think at all?'

'He watches the bay. Sometimes I catch him whispering to himself. He still dresses himself. Winds his watch.'

'Time means a lot to him. He must know, then. Punctuality was always his creed. Never late for work. Do you remember how he used to swim every day? Summer and winter. I shiver now at the thought.'

'You were never one for sport.'

There is a rustle in the undergrowth. 'Tomkins,' I cry.

'Here!'

'You are romantic. Tomkins died four years ago!'

'Is it that long?'

'It's more like six years since you were home.'

'Oh Theresa, if it were only you I'd be home every six months, but it takes me months to pluck up the courage to visit them.'

'At your age!'

Our voices aren't carrying against the wind; we have extinguished the candles and switched on the electricity and the bushes interlocked in light and shade outside are like great brooms sweeping the earth.

'My wife divorced me finally, you know.' I raise my voice against the wind.

'You knew it would go that way. And your young men, do they write?'

'Of course not. Unless … Well Quentin's in Berkeley studying shop windows or something. You know what they're like in the States. Education's not the slog we went through.'

'It was easy for you.' Theresa leans out to pick a leaf from a laurel.

'And where has it all got me? Fat. Successful. Unloved.'

'You'll marry again?'

'No.'

In the semi-dark, Theresa's profile is like a bitten apple. I run my lips down her hair line.

'I went to Djakarta last year. For the second time. I couldn't believe it. I felt strange, like a cipher or something. As though I hadn't travelled there but had arrived by some sort of spiritual means. I don't even know why I went. I'd seen it all before, the seated Buddhas, the cyclamen terraces. But I'm talking too much. What about you. Your brother?'

'Solid as ever. Apart from the gout. Our spiritual disease.'

When she laughs I see that her teeth are false at last; her

skin is luminous as silk, however. It always was.

'Do you still go down to him?' I remember her brother as blunt and cagey. When younger he had been an engine driver with the most romantic attraction for me. But when he left the railways and went to work in the Swastika laundry I lost interest in him.

She says she hasn't seen him since my father got so feeble and I feel the old frissons of guilt riding up my spine.

'They are helpless,' she says and I wish she didn't read my mind so openly.

'Better my father had died before he lost the will to talk. They never knew, did they, what the other was thinking, feeling? The Protestant ethic. Never complain, just hide and the weak one gets devoured. Or about us?'

'Did you?'

'Yes, Theresa, yes. But did I understand my wife? I thought I did once. I thought I loved her.'

'But you didn't.'

'You know.'

She moves abruptly from the window and pulls the casement in. The curtains which had swollen into the room fall heavily as though talked into good behaviour and the room is suddenly close. Theresa in the electric glare once again white, stiff.

'Go into them now. We'll take a walk tomorrow. He has waited for you a long time.'

'Don't propitiate me, Theresa.' I feel anger now. Angry with the ageing processes that are coming between us, the irrelevance of my visit. I feel it would have been better if the sounds of the sea and wind had been the traffic on the King's Road in London. As I go to the door I turn to look at her. 'Are you still able for the hill?'

These unkindnesses are never deeply hidden inside me. She knows this as she tosses her head without answering, where another would have said, 'Damn you, damn you.'

CHAPTER THREE

JESS PATS THE SEAT FOR HIM to sit beside her. His sister is wrapped in rugs although the sun is high. There is a clatter of pots and pans and good smells coming from the basement. She has short dark hair cut in a deep fringe which makes her look younger than she is but her voice is older than her looks. This anomaly in her appearance makes him feel uncomfortable. Maria, however, prim as a hat pin, is sitting on the steps. Her hands are clasped round her knees, her too-long skirt folded over under them. She is fair, or pale mouse, the hair is thin and when she bends her head it falls to reveal her pale skull; everything about her speaks of disapproval; her mouth is perpetually pinched as she bites her long upper lip with her bottom teeth. Cedric is afraid of her although her voice is never raised in anger. However, now he is moved to shock and says so that she will overhear, 'And Theresa tells me a new family has moved in above and the daughter, Carmel I think, has just won a beauty competition.'

'They are very common. RC's.'

Cedric's laughter interrupts the distant sound of tennis balls hitting racquets. 'Have you met them yet?' deliberately addressing Jess.

'Ma won't allow it.'

And when Cedric says, 'I'll soon change that,' Maria gets up and goes into the house.

'She's very cross, isn't she? Growing up doesn't suit her.

'Pretty girls are scarce,' he continues. 'Does she emerge, her royal highness, to water the roses or paint them like in *Alice in Wonderland*?'

'*Through the Looking Glass*,' she says.

'Oh darling pedant.' But when Jess starts to cough he feels the familiar heat of wariness. She is dying perhaps. The grown-ups think so. Dying of consumption. Red spots on either cheek. Red roses. Death roses. For death, not love. He shuts his eyes and looks to the sun to warm his eyelids. A pleasure he always enjoys.

'Why, there's so much sky in Ireland.' His mind drills back to sweaty dressing rooms and hated Rugby football days, and more hated prep nights in a dust-bound library. Jess rustles the pages of her book. She coughs again and he sits up sharply, his body jerking over like a scythe.

'Damn it,' he shouts. 'Is there nothing they can do?'

'Pa's sending me to a sanatorium in Switzerland this autumn.' She chokes out the sentence and subsides back into her rugs. He pulls a fringe of one over her shoulder.

'Why, that's tremendous. You'll be fine. Fine. You'll get better there. Everyone does.' His overblown enthusiasm sends blood to his head. He feels dizzy; tiny tadpoles swim behind his eyelids.

'Did you get my letter of congratulation?' Jess is not taken in.

'Yes. Imagine. Oxford. It is a beautiful town. I'll write to you every day. Every day a different sensation. A different smell. A different person to meet. Intelligent people everywhere. Men who can teach you something instead of the fuggy masters I've been used to.' Jess sniffs.

'Don't you believe me? Jess, Jess, darling, it'll be you and me eventually. You'll see. When you're running around again and we share books and thoughts and *ideas*. And furthermore I'm going to call on the McDonnells today. Formally.' He waves his arms now in an arc like an African dancer.

'Not now. Ma's resting. *I* have to live here. If I were gone … then it wouldn't matter.' Now the smile and sniff simultaneously.

'Don't make me feel guilty, sweetheart. Please.'

So he has killed the conversation. He gets up and wanders into the house. From the drawing room window he watches Richard belting the ball at his twin brother James. James was lovely, the prettiest of them all as a child: golden curled, gap-toothed, squint-eyed, but secretive. Now he has gangled into adolescence. His shorts reach down to bony knees as he leaps from one foot to the other trying to return Richard's bull's-eye serves. But his face is fine and angular; he has yet to grow into his nose. The twins are three years his junior. Richard is podgy and puppyish as James is lanky. So two eggs got fertilised instead of one. They say twins skip a generation, he thinks with some relief.

Strange to look back to that memory of James's prettiness. Few of the Stewarts were good-looking in a lanky Anglo-Irish manner. Most of them inclined to boxiness; stubbiness of fingers with squashed faces and high cheekbones. Maria and James were the only two that could be described as in any way aristocratic-looking; both Ma and Pa had donated to Richard, Jess and himself a stocky, worthy sort of look, with noses inclining to broadness as well and heavy-lidded eyes (these from Ma).

'If Richard were to hit a ball into the neighbouring garden,' he thinks idly. 'Then … '

At that he runs out again and calls from the court, 'Who's winning?' James's monosyllabic 'Him' gives Cedric his chance. 'I'll give you a game after tea and you'll win six-love six-love. I don't have Richard's *frou* for ball games.'

The set is over and Richard meticulously winds down the net.

'Did you get your cap this term again?' Cedric panders to Richard.

'Played full-back for the first fifteen.'

'Well done. Well done. Come up and see my new collection; you'll be interested.' Richard plans to be a doctor when he grows up and Cedric knows he won't want to look at his treasures. 'I'm going to Giza this summer before going up to Oxford. If father allows it. I'll carve my initials on the Sphynx.'

Jess slaps her book shut. 'Don't forget to bring a ladder.'

Cedric doesn't know any more who's laughing at whom. It strikes him, and not for the first time, that the whole family lives on a plain where each one has a point for a stake from which he mustn't move and the game is: who can get the other to move first and consequently lose.

He walks away from them then, riddled with an astonishing grief. A grief that is different from his normal depression which goes and comes. Somehow he is aware that this grief is a positive thing and he must live with it for that is his lot. And no amount of scholarships or school prizes make any difference. He feels quite alone, empty as a bucket with a hole in it.

'Give me time, give me time,' he screams inwardly and wonders what he means. Perhaps he would have liked to go back into an earlier period ...

CHAPTER FOUR

T HE UNDERGROWTH IS ALIVE with children's voices. It is his tenth birthday. Maria is eleven going on twelve and she has arranged a paper chase for the older children who are already good readers. The folded papers are hidden here and there under gooseberry bushes, and one is in the hand of the scarecrow which flaps amongst the peas.

The Deweys and the Fitzgibbons are come from Greystones. Letitia Dewey is pretty.

Cedric's knees are raw behind from the rubbing of the rough material of his winter shorts, his long school socks sag over his calves. Every few minutes, it seems, he stoops to pull them up.

'You're with me,' Letitia squeaks. The Deweys are not shy, unlike the Stewarts. 'The Bartons can't come because they have German measles.'

'I know,' Cedric says, trying to keep calm while pulling up his socks.

'Do you learn French?' Letitia continues.

'Yes.' Cedric goes scarlet and drops his head.

'Come on, then. I know where the first clue is. I saw Maria hiding it.'

Cedric thinks this is cheating but says nothing. It is his first real sin and it damages him internally but he has to follow her.

'I say no words though I frighten the birds,' Letty reads and pulls him towards the scarecrow. 'Easy,' she squeals, gleeful, as she pushes Cedric to get the note. 'You reach up. You're taller than me.'

Another lie. Another sin. He reaches up in front of her and feels her soft hands ride up his waist. He jumps down and tucks in his shirt again. At his prep school they tell him girls are stupid; he wonders are they right. 'I'm not going on,' he says, now quite weak.

'Spoil-sport. Spoil-sport. Cowardy, cowardy custard, run away from mustard. Well I'm going on 'cos I'll win.'

'Bitch,' he shouts then. 'Bitch!'

'Oh, you naughty, naughty boy. I'll tell Mama.'

'Tell-tale tit,' he shouts back. But she has leapt out of the garden like a long-legged steer and is clattering down the gravel towards the grown-ups who are sitting in deckchairs sipping tea.

For the rest of the day Cedric lurks out of sight and it is not until late evening that he goes down to the kitchen.

Theresa is sitting in her usual chair, tired from the constant running of the day. The sobs which have choked him all day come out like an unplugged sink. Creeping on to her knee he gives in to this flood of despair. 'I didn't mean it, I didn't mean it. She kept on teasing, goading. She's horrid. I hope I never have another birthday. I hope I die before I'm eleven.' Theresa's cheeks like pansy petals press against his coarse burning skin.

'She's a stupid little faggot,' Theresa says quite un-ashamedly. 'Stuck-up.'

CHAPTER FIVE

WHY DID I BRING THAT UP? Did I ever play with that Dewey bitch again? I suppose she's some kind of faded beauty now. But thank heaven they moved away so I will probably never see her again.

Little girls want to kiss little boys. Big boys want to kiss big girls. Am I going off my head again? 'Theresa,' I shout. 'Theresa. For God's sake come up here and talk to me. I'm going loopy. All fifty-three years of me. Loopy. Loose as an old wino. Shuffling in mind like my father.'

Poor little Dewey creature really was making a pass at me. And I muffed it. But others never remember. What affects one seldom affects another. It would be an interesting experiment if a psychoanalyst got a whole lot of childhood friends together and found out what they remembered of each other. Each episode would be quite separate and not at all significant to the recipient of the hatred or love.

But it all swims upwards again to that afternoon with Richard and James. Jess, forlorn in her rugs but cruelly aware of his short-comings. Throwing his love back into his face. You can inflict any amount of pain on others when you're dying.

Cedric thinks of this now and files it away for the future. Yes, it was at ten that he experienced his first death-wish. But at eighteen, high cheekboned, black-haired, five foot ten, a little stocky, he cradles it again, that wish. In his room, calciferous with his sea treasures, he looks out at the McDonnell house: older, pre-Victorian – that short lacuna between Georgian and early Victorian – stone, but threatened with buttresses and ornate additions. Larger and more attractive than their own which was thrown together around the nineties, bow-windowed on the left (to the right an uncompromising small window) the drawing room – whose side faces the bay and the layered hill below.

The following day – week? – there was a Sunday. The same holidays certainly. That long grass-hoppered summer before Oxford. Cedric and the rest of the family are heading for church. The whole family traipses up the hill. But no. Because Cedric hears the phut phut of his father's Morris Minor as it scrunches out of the avenue. Jess sits in the dickie rugged to her nose. This is what she likes, feeling the fresh wind in her lungs. But shortly after the car passes he hears the scrunch of feet. The whole McDonnell family are returning from mass.

Carmel, who must be the beauty queen, turns out to be dark-haired. Her hair shines like ripe blackberries after rain. Her lips are wide, her teeth like film stars' – perfect. Her eyes are almond-shaped. All this Cedric thinks as he looks quickly at her. There are dozens of them it seems. Girls young, old and medium. All pretty, all jolly, loose-limbed, at ease.

But Carmel is marred by a gusty laugh. This she emits now at the sight of these down-at-heel Protestants. Cedric becomes overconscious of his family's clothes: Maria's grey silk coat and skirt and her cloche hat, not to mention his own dull fawn 'summer' suit, with Richard and James in their blazers and long shorts, Mother shapeless as a tree-trunk in her eternal black.

The Stewart family skirt the McDonnells as though they were on fire, hurrying and shuffling along the dry shore which runs down each side of the steep hill. Their heads are lowered, psalters tightly clutched to their breasts as though in fear of contamination by a holy Roman glance. Cedric, however, takes a squint at Carmel and her sisters. They do not cling to their clothes but allow them to dangle as an adjunct to their bodies; unlike themselves who are tortured by bodily sin and clutch everything around them, especially the girls who embrace their own breasts whenever approached.

When they are gone he turns; their giggling backs scorch him with shame; he wants to scream 'We're not monsters … we really aren't. Just buried in generations of Victorian morality, like mummies, stiff, swathed … Please, please talk to us.'

But he merely scrapes the pebbles with the toe of his shoe, hangs back until his mother shouts, 'Cedric dear, we'll be late … '

What follows church is almost worse: a 'chat' with Father. Yes, it is the same afternoon; sporadic lumps of cirrus keep dimming the sun. He climbs that old copper beech – a habit from early childhood, a place to escape the prying grown-up eyes – with his book. There in an elbow he cradles himself, book on knees, the mild breeze shaking the leaves and allowing little motes of larvae to scatter on the pages. But his thoughts won't concentrate. He is all the time conscious of the McDonnell house above on the hill. He sees himself kissing, squeezing Carmel in front of all the family. Declaring a mad passion, a desire – her down on the drawing room carpet in front of his mother, father, sisters, brothers until wild screams break forth and the whole family keels over in united shock. At the thought he laughs aloud. How would they go? Mother first, of course, clutching her chest, calling for Theresa. His brothers: 'I say, old man, aren't you going a bit far?' Maria: 'Disgusting.' Father: 'After all I've sacrificed … '

'Yes, Father?'

The old man stands at the foot of the tree.

'I'd like a word with you.'

Awkwardly Cedric descends, jumping the last few feet and landing in front of him.

They stand face to face, although this is an anomaly because Father never looks you in the eye. He addresses you as though there were a third person behind you who is taking notes and will afterwards remind you of the force of his meaning.

'You've done well. I'm very pleased with you.' His father's face is askew, or perhaps he is watching his son's hair because the latter now only offers his skull to the fullness of the father's gaze.

'Thank you, Father,' he mutters into his shirt.

'Have you thought of your plans?'

'Plans?'

'When you have graduated?'

'It's a long way off.' Cedric lifts his head. 'Shall I get a rug for you, Father? Would you like to sit on the grass?'

'I'm going to take a walk.' True. His dog, a wire-haired fox terrier, is making short 'fetch it' runs, lifting its snout expectantly every few yards to gaze back at his father's face.

'But before I go ... '

'Er ... yes, Father?'

'A young man starting his studentship should have a clear idea of how he'll follow through.'

'As much as I've thought of it at all I might consider the Indian Civil Service. I'd like to improve my knowledge of Hindu and Moslem art.'

'If you take this up I hope you'll take your duties seriously. Not treat your career as a hobby.'

'Yes, of course.' There is a silence twisting its rude tail around them both till Cedric blurts, 'I was wondering if you wouldn't mind if I spent that money you mentioned in your, er, letter, on a trip to Egypt before the Michaelmas term begins. I thought it'd be a good thing to bone up on the pyramids as they'd say at Rugby – that's if they'd say anything at all on the subject.' And then positing what must be his most vibrant plea, 'I want to be an historian.'

The father takes this up very quickly with an almost audible chuckle. 'At your age I was content to steer my studies into their predestined channels. Like your grandfather I should prefer you to follow one of the professions. Medicine or the law. Just having a vague desire to travel is, well, natural at your age, but only as an interlude. Your duty lies with your family, your church.'

'Richard is determined to study medicine. Surely one doctor in the family is enough.' Cedric tries to be light-hearted but his father doesn't smile. 'I wouldn't lose my allegiance to you or Mother if I went to Peking or Kyoto. Anyway for the moment I am entering Oxford. My scholarship allows me forty pounds a year. I'll be able to manage without your help. You'll need all your money if Richard is to be put through medical school and Jess goes to Switzerland.'

'I've always been correct in my dealings with my sons. It has not been some little sacrifice keeping you three boys at public schools and Maria at Cheltenham.'

'But why, Father, did you do it? I could just as easily have been educated here. It's snobbish nonsense having us sent to English schools.' Cedric feels the blood draining from his face as he says this. Never, never in all his dealings with his father has he dared to gainsay him like this. But he is angry, too; he trembles from terror. But he must keep his anger.

His father turns on his heel calling his dog, 'Come along, little doggie, then.' But just as Cedric feels the constriction in his chest easing off he turns back. 'I've decided to allow you sixty pounds a year which will bring your income up to one hundred pounds. I think you'll find that sufficient.'

Cedric's 'No', is a silent oval in his mouth. As is the scream that never bursts forth.

Yes, the sweat is on my palms now as I think of that moment.

Why did I say that, why? It must have made him so unhappy. Does he still remember it as he clutches the curtains like a baby clutching its soother? Is that why *he's* grown silent now? Is that why he doesn't recognise me?

'For God's sake, Theresa,' I shout out loud, 'come and talk to me … '

Years later I saw that picture by Edvard Munch, *The Scream*, and the full memory of that moment flew back into my consciousness never to be forgotten.

And all the while they are talking he's aware of a commotion going on in the neighbour's garden. Carmel and a young man are sitting on a rug not far from the dividing fence. He is tickling her ear with a piece of grass and her gusty laugh spreads over the hill. The boy's efforts to kiss her, he's also greedily noticed, are being repulsed by the girl. Each time he reaches over she pulls away and giggles. Now that his father has gone the game gets his full attention. His voyeuristic pleasure is doubled when suddenly a thrust makes her topple sideways and her skirt flies up her thighs, although it's with a sense of relief that he hears their tea-gong battling its way through the undergrowth. They jump up simultaneously, she rumpling down her clothing, and they run laughing up the hill until they are out of sight on the plateau above which must be their lawn. It is like a table to a baby, just above eye level.

CHAPTER SIX

'WHAT ON EARTH'S THE MATTER with you?' Theresa has appeared at the bottom of the stairs and is standing, minute and white.

'Here,' I say, 'sit here.' I pat the stair. 'I'm mad. Round the bend. I'm going insane.'

'That's tautology ... and stupid,' she says climbing slowly. 'Did you have another row?'

'Of course, of course. What else?'

'For God's sake can't you leave them alone? Have you no cop-on?'

'No.'

'Your father is nearly eighty-five and your mother's not much less.'

'She's a good ten years younger and strong as a bull.'

'So are you.'

'All right. Now. What'll I do? Call for the men in the white coats?'

'Don't be daft.'

'Hold my hand.'

CHAPTER SEVEN

IT SEEMS CEDRIC IS VERY MUCH at ease later on. He is sitting on the deal table in the kitchen; his sandshoes swing back and forth under the billow of his old grey flannels. Theresa, as pretty as a plum, makes tea in the delph teapot, scalding it first and replacing it on the range for just a minute after filling it with the boiling water.

'Well, they've all changed greatly since my last holidays. Except Ma and Pa of course. Richard is enormous with his ambitions. Grown too. Like a eunuch.'

'His blood hasn't thinned yet,' Theresa says, testing the tea in a used cup first for colour. 'Just right.'

'Just right? It's the colour caramel. Give me a cup!'

'Next term his manliness will have worn off, one hopes.'

'You're possibly right. But James! He's more secretive than ever.'

The tea cools. His hand, already sprouting tiny golden hairs, stretches out for a warm-up. 'What goes on in that sullen head?'

Cedric digs into the ambivalence of his feelings. 'I like him. A lot. But he doesn't reciprocate anyone's feelings. Mine, yours, Jesse's, Ma's ... of course ... '

CHAPTER EIGHT

CEDRIC FEELS THE COT RAILS constricting his movements. He has climbed up and stands clutching the bar
with his tiny fists. The bedclothes billow under him, they
sway; his small feet are like a raft riding the waves on Killiney
beach. He bellows. Ma appears suddenly out of the darkness,
candle in hand.

'Stop crying, you naughty boy … '

Cedric wants to see the new babies but is not allowed. He
has heard that Ma may give one away to a wet nurse. And
Cedric doesn't want this unknown and unseen new brother
to go to a wet nurse. 'She'll surely drown him,' he thinks
but is afraid to warn Mother. He is afraid of Mother.
Mortally afraid. 'Or make him cold.' It's cold to be always
wet.

He can't stop crying. Mother slaps him over and over. He
screams more. Mother calls, 'Theresa.'

When Theresa comes Ma says, 'Cedric is being very
naughty.'

Cedric holds his breath till Ma goes.

'What's a wet nurse, Th'resa, what's a wet nurse?' he
moans between the gulps of the dry sobs. Theresa takes him
out and hugs. Theresa tries to explain.

'Your mother can't feed both the babies.'

'But there's plenty of food in the house. Theresa, don't let
Ma give James away.' For somehow or other he knows it'll

be the weakly one. He's heard the grown-ups say that James is weakly. Ma doesn't want James.

CHAPTER NINE

'YES, SHE NEVER WANTED HIM.'
Theresa goes on to tell him that one of Jess's lungs is nearly gone but that she pretends she doesn't know how bad she is.

'She takes pleasure in her books.'

'I know,' Cedric says, wanting now to hug Theresa, but unable to. 'I'm not much use,' he adds lamely.

He moves deliberately away from her as she bends over to poke the range. The loud scatter of the coals creates a mysterious barrier between them. Later he would have realised that this was Theresa's self-protection. Whenever her emotions get the better of her – even now – she embarks on some noisy action. She always has been a very quiet person. Outside noise is a wall to hide behind.

CHAPTER TEN

JAMES, ABOUT SIX, IS LARKING ABOUT in the grass alone. He is trying to catch a butterfly. Cedric has been watching him enviously from the window. Why enviously? Why? Because he wants to play, puppy-like, with James. He has never touched his elder sister and baby Jess is too fragile for his uncollected limbs.

'James!' he shouts from the window. 'Can I play with you?'

A deep scowl spreads over the golden surface of James's face. He doesn't answer but runs into the house, banging the front door behind him.

CHAPTER ELEVEN

'WHO ELSE CAN WE DISCUSS?' Cedric says when Theresa has finished stirring the fire.

'Maria is unhappy, I think,' Theresa says.

'Weird ...

'He must have been afraid I'd tell on him for chasing the butterfly ... ' Cedric continues.

'What on earth are you talking about?'

'I was thinking of an incident when I was about nine.' Cedric describes the incident but goes back abruptly to Maria. 'Yes, weird.'

'To you,' Theresa says, rather sharply. 'Her only pleasure is in the hunt. Her face lights up those wintry mornings.'

But Cedric is too insolent, too shut away in his emotions which veer between sex and academia – but then, to Cedric, nudity was art – to think of pleasure in the shape of following a drag hunt over Calary bog on a horse. 'Just weird, I repeat, and don't show your disapproval, Theresa darling.'

Now they can hug, with friendship so long associated with touch; mutual laughter runs over their breasts, the thrust and smell of each other, to each the greatest protection of all.

Later, on the stair, I heard Mother call. I bumbled into her room. I remember I was struck by its shrine-like appearance –

a room long consecrated by my father to disuse and awe. Mother looked like a sluttish old virgin in her powder blue nightie and wispy unbunned hair trailing over the pillow. Fortunately she didn't want me; she thought my step was Richard's and I was able to retreat before we entered into argument. I remember thinking then, James was the best off. Mother and Father treated him as if he weren't there. Oh, to be invisible, I remember feeling.

Days, weeks went by and he was no nearer meeting Carmel McDonnell nor gauging his future through the heavy tomes in which his mind tried to bury its defenceless self. It was blue and grey and gold that summer. Luminous as a Van Gogh one minute, the next vague and exquisite as a Turner and then there was that day – and afternoon when everything changed.

As usual the bleak kitchen is the setting: the scrubbed tiles, the four deal chairs, the deal table, the delph teapot, the kitchen mugs, the half-light from the windows, the clatter of Ellen the maid, the ironing board with the scorched mark of the iron on the cloth. Since they got 'the electric' the old flat irons had been thrown out and a suave electric iron which stood up on its end had replaced them. But that didn't prevent various maids from burning most of the clothes and when one went out one was at pains to disguise these areas of disaster.

'What's the good of having a scholarship?'

'Always moaning.'

'But I was so excited when I heard, I thought I'd fly. But now I might as well be recovering from the measles.'

'I wrote, didn't I?' Theresa says, brushing crumbs from under me.

'And Jess wrote, I admit. But hey, I'm fed up with the McDonnell situation. Every time I try to intercept her – on the hill, on the beach, going to church – she looks at me as though I smelled. And that nasty looking oaf she knocks about with. They're doing a line, I suppose.'

Theresa bursts out laughing, 'A line?' And Ellen puffs into giggles.

'What's so funny about that?'

'The way you say it. You look so mournful.'

'Well, I am mournful. Goddam fed up. He's like a draper's assistant with his mincing little ways.'

'Snob!' Theresa says.

'Here, Ellie,' Cedric says, swivelling round, 'give us a kiss!'

'Tomorrow,' Ellie says, squirming out of reach.

'Guess what! I'm telling lies. I did talk to her and … ' a dramatic pause … 'I kissed her!'

'You did, did you? And what did she do? Throw a pail of water over you?'

'Ask Theresa. She knows.' But Theresa has gone into the pantry and is banging saucepans about. 'Theresa! Come back and listen to me!' He gets up – a little forlorn, like one who has mislaid something precious. 'Are you not interested in my amorous pursuits?' He has entered the pantry and stands behind her, his hands slowly rising to her shoulders.

'Not in the least!' she doesn't turn.

'Well kiss me then. *You* kiss me!'

Was it then? I search frantically in the tail of my memory, looking sideways at her profile. Was it then I took this face in my hands and said, 'You are beautiful'? Was it then that my adulthood stepped out of its attic where it had been waiting for me all those years? Of course it was, because all against Ellie's storm of laughter my body felt a sort of quilted languidness. I can hold it now in my memory, as who can't hold the memory of their first kiss?

★

The electric moments are followed by those of surprise, astonishment even. Ellen who is riveted is told to leave the room and Theresa goes back to the sink to batter the delph as though in punishment for the unexpected depths of her own feelings. And then he is embarrassed; has he inexorably stepped beyond the barriers of their controlled but intimate relationship, slipped into a seam of sexual encounter which should have been reserved for someone younger, hopefully stupid and from which he can easily extricate himself? With an effort he comes back to earth with, 'But God, doesn't he understand that I admire him? God! It's so easy to hate him but I'm senseless to hate him. I might as well be six years old and told I'm not to go down to the beach alone. He drones on with his ambiguities punctuated by those awful silences.'

And then suddenly, 'Sorry Theresa.'

'For what?' she merely says, her back still to him.

He feels sullen, awkward as a twelve-year-old finding himself alone with a girl for the first time. She says then, more softly, 'I understand.'

He feels an enormous spread of relief running over his body, hot and sticky as it is from nervous exposure.

'So now there's this and this,' he says, 'no more silences, no more terror. Perhaps no more church, being preached at in empty vowels that come from nowhere. Why do clergymen all put on that hoop-like tone when addressing their flock?'

'Our lot are the same. Sententious buggers.'

'Oh, my love, my love,' he is cool again, now, can return to the fondling tones with which he used to address her without feeling embarrassed. 'Do they talk like that? Opening their mouths as though they were swallowing olives all the time. Making us feel uneasy just for the sake of it?'

'Because they are mostly so pitifully inadequate themselves.'

'Mr Pike is a real blister ... ' He pulls himself up quickly, aware that he must get rid of public school mouthings once and for all. 'Old fogey ... ' He tries to resign himself to the type of speech he's adopted in advance – he hopes – for the courtship of Carmel.

Can he?

'When I suggested to Father that I'd like to go east you'd think I'd suggested starting a brothel in Killiney.'

The music of Theresa's laughter rings through beamed kitchen and pantry. 'I'd like to see it.' They are the same height now – he an inch or two taller perhaps – and he wants to hug her again, although afraid he may not re-encounter the amazement of levitation that that first kiss instilled in him: also he is too shy now, he has to leave the room.

CHAPTER TWELVE

THAT NIGHT IN HIS ROOM he idles, prowls, sits, sorts his marine collection, never staying at one thing for long, his thoughts like musical notes running up and down the chromatic scale. When after a thunderous knocking Richard and James enter he is faced with his two brothers, the one caustic, arrogant, the other shifting; he realises that nothing has changed after all. His back straightens, 'Yes?'

Richard points to a crusty sponge, 'Look, James, Cedric's going to start washing at last. Ha ha ha.'

Cedric, small ledger in hand, ignores, pretends to be immersed in his notes. James says, pointing to a minute cowrie shell, 'That's pretty, a secure little object, full of sea and safety.'

'Sissy,' Richard cries, giving James a shove.

'I should have thought,' Cedric says, a dryness emptying his mouth, 'that a potential doctor should have been interested in marine biology.'

'Very interesting, very ... Sea-wrack, bladder-wrack. Those are dead weeds.'

'So what.' Cedric snaps his ledger shut and goes to the door.

'But it is interesting, Richard,' James insists, taking with delicate fingers a sea-horse and holding it up to the parsimonious bulb.

'Leave it, leave it.' Richard again shoves his brother who

nearly rocks the glass cabinet on to its head. The little horse cracks into powder.

Cedric's rage now clamours like a fire-brigade's siren. But it is all inside his head. At last he emits the word 'Out', snatching open the bedroom door. Again, 'Out!' This time the word oddly high like the quavering top C of an ageing tenor.

The twins hover in a glaring silence till Richard manages, 'Yes, old chap, you're right. Let's go, James, the room pongs. Smells. Suits him down to the ground.'

He is degraded; degraded by his self-love, his being so ingrown. He wishes to beat the cabinet with his fists. He stands with his back against the door and unbuttons his flies. Quite soon, the sperm spills ivory tadpoles onto his trousers; faint with apprehension he backs out and runs to the bathroom, wiping, wiping, his hand a young lamb's pink on the grey of his flannels; the bathroom window flapping in the wind, steps that come and go along the corridor and he must get back. Get back to his room without being seen.

In his room again he climbs on his bed and secures a book from the shelf. The photograph of Maria and Jess on the swing falls from the leaves. He gazes at it vacantly. His bed is at the window and he crawls over, his chin on the sill. He points his Brownie at the McDonnell house. The garden is empty of life, insects tucked up for the night, sheets of moonlight making the flower beds a uniform black. The house leans against the hill, a window here and there is lighted on the second storey, and there is a gush of electricity from the large downstairs room, the windows wide open, the curtains undrawn. He can see heads above chintz, a piano, an embroidered stool. The furniture is less solid, more ornate, than their own. A red carpet (bad taste?) blazes across the floor. He clicks his camera, knowing the photo will not come out but in some way satisfy a kind of humorous statistic which he feels may come in handy in later years.

CHAPTER THIRTEEN

IS HE OBSESSED NOW? He follows Theresa wherever she goes, touches her gingerly from time to time; they laugh a lot. That summer it seems she has become miraculously young (she is in fact thirty-one); she smells of cotton when he bends to take the bucket of slop from her, out of his mother's room; he catches the worn wooden handle of the pail and feels the warmth of her hand on it. Sometimes he burns his fingers deliberately on the iron frying pan while helping her with the breakfast in order that she may catch his cuff and drag him to the sink to salve the burn under the cold tap. The tall taps stand like soldiers on either side of the sink; the sink has a myriad of brown cracks; it is as big as a trough. In the musty corridor that runs beyond the kitchen and up the steps out the back door he longs to kiss her but daren't (to this day that passage strikes me as dangerous). But at night in his hard bed, the sheets rumpled from tossing, he thinks of Carmel McDonnell's overgrown adolescent breasts and fondles his penis.

There is a subtle division in his mind. Love equals kissing – lust equals the other thing, tunnelled into his mind in sweaty dormitories, cold dressing-rooms, on the sportsfield. The kiss. 'The kiss,' he often mutters to himself.

Then again on other days, his gramophone under the chestnut tree, he is absorbed in the divisions and numbers of Beethoven whom he has just discovered; he imagines the

music as increasing in circles like water disturbed by a pebble
or a rising fish. Sometimes Jess trailing her rug sits heavily
beside him, her short nose raised, the sniff withheld, and they
share for a short while the lofty extravaganza of one of the
later symphonies.

But strangely it is a day like many another when Cedric
suddenly decides on a plan. It is a Saturday afternoon when
the bumble-bees hover over the phloxes and the Stewarts all
scattered about the lawn browse at their thoughts or their
books that he quietly gets up and goes into the house. He
fetches a glossy magazine from Ellen's room, a learned tome
from his own, and casually, as though he does the same thing
every day, emerges from the house once more, skirts the
lawn and cutting through the kitchen garden runs down the
hill to the railway line. Ducking under the wire, he climbs
the wall and jumping from it rolls in the sand that crusts the
edge of the stony beach like demerara sugar.

He doesn't have to wait long because they round the
railway café quite soon. Carmel's swain carries the parapher-
nalia of a badminton set, racquets tucked under his arm, and
Carmel carries a picnic basket of orange straw. The young
man busies himself erecting the net and makes a half-hearted
attempt to sweep away the worst of the stones as he marks
the playing field with his heel. Carmel spreads herself on the
pebbles, her pleated white skirt opened like a fan over her
legs, and begins to attack the basket.

'Let's have a game first,' the boy implores. Cedric notices
with satisfaction that he overlays a Dublin accent with open
vowels that don't belong. Neither of them has as yet seen
him; he pretends to read.

She has got up now and stands expectant, racquet in hand,
as though she were on the centre court at Fitzwilliam. He
thinks she looks presentable like this – quite athletic, in fact
– her black hair is pinned into a plait at the back and her
wide face and high cheekbones accentuated. She dives and

jumps for the ball awkwardly negotiating the pebbles until with a frivolous 'Ow' she sinks to the ground.

Cedric leaps to his feet and runs towards her, sinking to his knees in a theatrical curve – he hasn't missed his cue – and his hand comes quickly to rest on her foot. 'Excuse me interfering, but my brother is studying medicine. You must have this seen to at once.' While he speaks he deftly winds his handkerchief round her ankle and heel in a figure of eight. 'That'll support it for now. You have to be very careful with a sprain. A sprain is often more painful than a fracture. Also when you think you've only sprained your ankle there could easily be a fracture as well. That's why it's wise to have an x-ray. But I don't think this is too serious.' He twists the foot this way and that. 'Hurt?' Carmel makes an effort to screw her face into an agonised pout but bursts out laughing. 'It has rather spoiled your game, I'm afraid.' Squinting into the luminous sky he catches a scowl of amazement on the boyfriend's face. 'Sorry I'm not much good or I'd give you a game while ... she ... rests. By the way I'm Cedric Stewart. Your next-door neighbour. We pass, occasionally, on the road.' A little laugh lifts out of him, 'I've often wanted to say hullo but I'm too strictly brought up to ... well, importune people to whom I haven't been formally introduced. Forgive me, I'll leave you in peace now.'

'Oh no, please,' Carmel says. 'As you know, you silly, I'm Carmel, your neighbour also!'

'Well of course I knew. I hear you've just won a competition. Congratulations.'

'It's silly, really. My mother sent in my photo and then five of the entrants were sent for, for the judging. It was awful! I never thought I'd get the prize. The other girls were much prettier.'

'You just think that because you are a nice modest girl.' He appraises the curve of her calf, imagines the muscles spreading further upwards. He's pleased to see she's a strong limbed young woman; he hates pulpy females.

'Are you the eldest?' Carmel asks, now seated legs spread in a V, her hands untucking the picnic fare.

'My sister Maria's the eldest. Then myself. Then the twins and Jess is at the bottom of the ladder.'

'Is she the one that always sits with a rug spread over her knees?'

'Yes, she's got TB. Consumption.'

'Gracious, that's awful.'

'It is. Especially as she's the only one with any substance.'

'I wouldn't like to have that,' Carmel says, not quite taking his meaning correctly.

She begins to smear raspberry jam on a piece of bread and butter.

'You look in the pink of health. The way you danced on the pebbles. Quite nimble. And graceful.'

Carmel's face glows. 'Don't be shy,' Cedric continues, offering a fatherly hand on her shoulder. 'Haven't you got your prize to prove it?'

'It's only a silly old competition.'

Carmel now goes on to describe her gradual climb up the ladder of success. How the girls were sorted, reduced to five in number. How three judges, characterised by their mutual prurience, lowered over the unfortunate entrants.

'I felt like Bran – my dog, that is – at the Ballsbridge show,' Carmel says, 'parading up and down. Each one of us did it. At first I didn't care whether I won or not but then at the last moment I was mad keen. Funny, isn't it?'

Cedric whistles through his teeth in approbation. He's enjoying himself more than he expects. 'We all go through that sort of thing some time in our lives. I experienced a similar sort of volte-face, turn around, when I sat for the Oxford scholarship. At first when the headmaster put my name up I thought: 'Heavens I don't want to go to Oxford. More studying!' Because I'm really very lazy. Then when

I'd actually done the exam – I think there were quite a few others as well – I was all keyed up. In a terrible state of nerves. I think I'd have died of shame if I hadn't won.'

'You won! Hey, George! Do you hear that? Cedric's going to Oxford.' The boyfriend, now George, is trying to camouflage his chagrin behind a mouthful of bread and chicken paste; he snorts and little crumbs come shooting out of his lips.

To make matters worse Cedric digs in the basket and produces a paper napkin and says with a disarming (already practised at great length in the mirror at home) shrug, 'It's nothing, really. Now. At the time it seemed as though the gates of heaven had been opened. But now. Well it's like a dream. Especially with my family.'

'I love my family.'

'Perhaps they're more relaxed than mine. Mine are very snobbish.'

'You're not snobbish.'

Cedric wonders now about this game, aware that there might be religious reservations on her family's side as well but he takes it on a peg. 'There's no point in being snobbish. But tell me more. What happened after the judging?'

'Well, everyone shook hands and I was handed a cheque for ten pounds. Ten pounds! Can you imagine? Ooh, the mound of things I've bought with it already. I bought this,' she smoothes her skirt over her legs; 'do you like it?'

'It's lovely.'

It is inconceivable though true that George has not opened his mouth once – except to splutter crumbs – during the whole interchange between Cedric and Carmel, although the latter seems to take this as natural. 'And the badminton set. As a present for my sister, really, but we're just borrowing it for the afternoon. The others have gone to lunch in Blackrock. Which reminds me, aren't you missing your dinner? Bread and jam isn't much.'

'Who cares. And then?'

'Well then I went to tea in Mitchell's with the three judges. Awfully nice. They bought me everything I fancied: scones, tea cakes, macaroons.' Cedric nearly yawns but blows his nose in time. 'Would you like to come to tea with us today?' This is different.

'Yes,' he says with alacrity. 'But … of course. What time?'

'Mum says tea is very elastic. Any time between four and five. I'll get Annie to make a chocolate cake. Annie's a wonderful cook. How many maids have you?'

'Theresa and she's different. Not a maid really. She came to nurse me when she was sixteen and she's stayed ever since. There's only Ellie, really, and she's a funny slut. Funny. Fun. Is Ellie.'

'We have three. Oh, I don't mean to boast. Annie does the cooking and there's Percy.'

'Percy?'

'Yes, he's Annie's son. He does the dirty work. And there's Rose. She's pretty. But she drops everything.'

Cedric by now realises the shores of difference between the two families. Not only would a maid who 'dropped everything' be sacked in his household but there'd never be a Percy. He wishes suddenly for a Percy on whom, like on the shoulders of the coachmen in old Russia, children had wept and been comforted. Although he did have Theresa and the thought of her suddenly in all this basking in Carmel's casual warmth causes his heart to tighten in an unfamiliar way.

'You must come,' Carmel insists now, 'and meet the others.'

'I'm more keen on meeting you again.'

'The others, my younger sister especially, are much nicer than I am.'

'They couldn't be. You're the nicest girl I ever met.' Which is true, Cedric thinks, for the first time aware that everything is not after all planned by the great Cedric, the logician.

But this emphatic statement causes George to speak: 'Let's go.'

'But why, George? We haven't finished our picnic yet.'

'Actually I'd better go myself. I was wondering … if … would you like to come to tea with me in Dublin … some time … this week … We could take the tram from Westland Row somewhere or walk up to Robert Roberts. They have an orchestra there. Three funny ladies playing "The Blue Danube" and stuff like that. A violin, a cello and a piano. Would you like that?'

'Ooh that would be lovely.'

'Perhaps we might do a theatre or the cinema. I'll consult the papers and see what's on!'

'I'm sure that'd be all right. Especially when Daddy knows it's you.'

'Have you ever been in an aeroplane?'

It's too late to retract, and Cedric plunges on.

'Well there was a chap in school whose father had one. And he invited me down. But unfortunately he couldn't get the damn thing off the ground the day I was there. Something went wrong with the prop or something.' Mortified now at the return of his public school jargon he jumps to his feet.

'Don't mind me. See you this afternoon.'

'About half past four.'

CHAPTER FOURTEEN

Bᴜᴛ ᴄᴇᴅʀɪᴄ ʜᴀs ᴛᴏ ʀᴜɴ ᴛᴏ ᴛʜᴇʀᴇsᴀ before he goes. Anywhere. Everywhere. 'Oh Theresa, Theresa.' Yes, he is shouting her name now; his voice can be heard all over the house; like a clutch of chickens running wild from the pen. 'Theresa, Theresa … ' Into the bedrooms, the scullery, the kitchen.

'What's got into you?' Ellie has her broad arms up to the elbows in suds.

'I must see Theresa.'

'Theresa, Theresa, Theresa. What are you going to do without her when you leave home for good?'

'Shut up, will you? I must see her.'

'She's above.'

'Above where?' Oh, agony, he's already searched the bedrooms. At the door, he tearing out, she walking in stately, with his mother's tray in her arms.

'Mind, mind, mind.'

'Not mind,' Cedric gasps.

At times like these Cedric feels the Christ-like simplicity that Theresa long ago imposed on him, an agony which is nearly impossible to bear. Later, the frequently attempted suicides for which he blamed largely his non-relationship with his father, his hatred of his mother, perhaps stemmed from his inability to live up to this. But at that moment he must think only of Carmel and the forthcoming tea party in the McDonnell household. He blurts now, 'I met Carmel on the beach. She's asked me to tea this afternoon. She's a really nice girl, not at all stuck-up.'

'What did you expect her to have, two heads? Oh you Stewarts,' Ellen says, risking a reproof from Theresa.

'But what am I going to tell Mother? She'll come down on me like a ton of bricks. And Jess particularly. She'll get the brunt.'

'Think of yourself for a change,' Theresa bluntly says. 'Jess won't get the blame if she knows nothing. I'll think up something. I'll say you are taking a long walk and won't be back till supper. You will be back then?'

Theresa's overenthusiastic plans worry Cedric. He thinks she minds and is not sure why. Does she also not approve of the Stewarts meeting the McDonnells? How absurd but also possible.

'You don't want me to go. You can't hide things from me.'

'That's what I used to say to you.'

These implications have a new importance to Cedric now, just gone eighteen and in the wedge between a distant English public school and Oxford. When Theresa says now, 'She's very pretty and I'm sure she's sweet too,' he remembers everything very clearly. That is to say he knows suddenly why he has felt such ambivalence since his return from the beach. He puts his hand on Theresa's shoulder to knead the cotton that covers her flesh.

'Theresa, when I was about five or six I fell off a branch of a tree and I was terrified. I wasn't supposed to climb it. It was against the rules and I was terrified I'd broken my leg or something. I just lay there bawling in a pitiful state. So what happened? Theresa came running out of the house and brought me down to the kitchen, she gave me a cup of tea (also against the rules) and she felt all down my legs and you called the doctor, saying you were sick. And then you casually mentioned that I'd had a bit of a fall but not to mention it to my parents. And I remember thinking that I wished you and I could live alone in some little house where my parents would never find me again. Do you remember? Well, that night you brought me a hot drink and sat on my bed for ages. You were like a little girl. You must have been nearly as young as I am now. Well, do you remember what you told me?'

'Some nonsense probably.'

'Well I'll tell you. You told me about a young man that you were walking out with in Ballybrack. You described him as "A decent sort of fellow with a rather down-trodden look" but that he wanted to marry you. And I could have died. Do you know that I could have died? I wanted to kill him. I used to lie in bed night after night thinking of Pa's shotgun and how I'd pepper him with bullets! Can you believe it? At six years old?'

'I didn't marry him.'

'Why didn't you?'

'Even when you were six you were more fun to talk to than he was. He was a right bloody fool!' They are now laughing and hugging over their equal memory.

'Did he ever tell you you were beautiful?'

'Me?'

'Shall I tell you?'

'At my age?'

'How old are you?'

'Thirty-one.'

'You don't look it.'

'When you're eighteen most of the world is a very old place and most of the people in it.'

'You are beautiful. And I know that. But promise me you'll never marry a bloody fool.'

'And what would you do if I did?'

'I'd shoot him. I'm not joking.'

'I'm sure you would.'

'And another thing. I don't think Carmel is particularly intelligent. Not half as intelligent as you. But she's easy to talk to. You can say anything to her. Not like here where really I can't talk to anyone – except you of course. Not even Jess although I try very hard with her. And another thing. I've never been in a Catholic household before. Can you believe it? I'll be able to write this earth-shattering experience down in my diary tonight. Just think of it! "Tea with McDonnells. They are Catholics." Have you cheered me up now?'

'Yes.'

'And you know you are beautiful?'

'If you say so.'

CHAPTER FIFTEEN

T HE McDONNELLS' TEA PARTY marked a notch in my life, I suppose; the conversation round the table was like a collection of teasing dots. 'How wonderful!' 'Oxford!' 'What a fine hard-working man your father is.' And afterwards, hot and sticky from the tea, Carmel persuaded me to see 'the rest of the house'.

Cedric asks her has she ever been to a dance and she says only a school dance. 'Have you?' She is a bit confused now, climbing the majestic stairs (more majestic than the stairs at home). They are in a room now with a piano – Blüthner drawing room grand – and Cedric wonders, not for the first time, what Mr McDonnell does for a living.

'Do you play?' he asks, noticing the cut asters in a not very valuable vase. He thinks suddenly that his mother is very Victorian: she drops, for example, the 'h' in hospital, says vause for vase; and Mrs McDonnell is an Edwardian but not a suffragette like his elder sister Maria. Struck by this he turns the notion over and over in his mind. He must mean, he thinks, that Maria would have been if she had been born earlier in the century; now she is merely mannish, discontented.

Carmel rattles on: 'Do you think I could persuade Mummy to throw a ball on my eighteenth birthday?'

She does not play the piano, she says, 'Unfortunately, but my sister Evelyn does.' She wishes she did. 'That's the parents' bedroom. We can't go in there. Do your parents sleep in the same room?'

'They must have, four times at least!'

And Carmel says, 'Do you know, you're funny.'

'In what way?'

'Don't know. But you are. Perhaps it's because of your scholarship.'

'You mean it's like a disease?'

'Don't know. Is it?'

'Yes it is. But it's not the scholarship really. It's probably being at a boarding school that has unhinged me.'

'What does that mean?'

'Sent me mad, slightly.'

'But you're not mad. You're very nice.' This latter blurted out with the accompanying flush.

They have reached the third floor: an open door, a puff of perfume. 'Where are we now?'

'You can come in.'

'Do you sleep here?'

'Why, is there something odd about it?'

'On the contrary. It's ... well ... queenly.' His own family, i.e. Jess and Maria, have cold austere rooms. 'Can I? Do I dare to sit on the bed?'

The eiderdown puffs disturbingly beneath his buttocks. For a while he's silenced in its comfort while Carmel stands in front of him. 'Imagine sleeping in a bed like this. The beds at home are like boards. The Romans never had pillows. Did you know that? In spite of the fact that they had a most advanced civilisation they had wooden pillows.'

'I don't believe it.'

'Neither do I, actually. It's the sort of thing that's rammed down your throat at boarding school. I'm sure people like Nero lolled about on cushions.'

'Nero? I had a dog called Nero once. He got run over.'

'Yes, lots of dogs get called Nero.'

'I cried when he went. So I got Bran. You haven't met him.'

'No, actually I haven't.'

'He's horrible but he talks. He licks my face when he wants anything.'

'Lucky him!'

There is a shy giggling from Carmel and she moves a little away.

'No. Come here.'

Yes, there was a scuffle, I remember. All the time Cedric pulling and she saying, 'No, someone might come.'

And then trying again: 'Are you going to marry George?'

'He's stupid. Of course not.'

And Cedric, hounded once more, says, 'They say that.'

'What do you mean?'

'Why do you encourage him?'

'He's the only one around. I wouldn't like to marry a stupid man. I'd rather marry a ... scholar.'

In the end he gets her down beside him and although she struggles, his skin is a furnace of desire. He fights for the straps of her summer dress whose cotton bodice prohibits with its tightness what he wants to squeeze in his hand. It is not languid like the kiss with Theresa, nor does he fly above the clouds, but it is all wild, hot, inevitable. Inevitable, that is, for he must finally jump off the bed and run to the window, leaving her to cry childishly, turning her head into the pillow, till jumping up she too is at the window beside him, saying 'What is the matter?'

CHAPTER SIXTEEN

I AM THINKING, PRIMARILY, of the Cedric at home in the cloistered shackles of his parents' house. Never away, studying, discovering mythologies, ghosts even; reading Goethe, Schiller, riding on the trail of Waugh, Lawrence, the Fabians; never at ease in the surroundings of Grantham, the Ox, punting. A bit of a solitary – politically left, of course, but unable to join any debating society. No, I'm not going to tell of those years, specifically, the whole of England conscious of the veil of Hitlerism obscuring the sky in western Europe. So I must guess, and it is not difficult, because much has been recounted to me by Theresa and Jess herself.

It must be the summer of 1939 because Ma and Pa are beside the wireless and Pa says, 'I don't know what Chamberlain is doing. It's no good putting it off any longer.'

Mother holds my letter in her hand and reads it out:

> I have received a double first in my final examination. Ancient History and English. You may not know but I had a slight breakdown earlier this year, therefore I am especially pleased with the results. I needn't tell you that I had some pretty awful moments during the exams. However all's well that ends well. I shall be stopping in London on the way home to visit the British Museum and look up a fellow student who has digs in Maida Vale. So

please do not expect me till the middle of July.

I hope that Jess is no worse for the dreadful winter that has passed and that the rest of the family, including yourself and Father, flourishes.

Your affectionate son,
Cedric.

Mother pauses to adjust her reading glasses and Father says, 'Isn't that splendid? Aren't you delighted, Edith?'

'Of course. It's so wonderful coming on top of Richard's news yesterday.'

'I must ring up Ridgeway. He has been most sympathetic with his enquiries lately.'

Mother attacks with, 'Does he want something from us?'

My father, weary to the bone from his long day at his office, says, 'Jack Ridgeway is a very old friend. I shall telephone him at once.'

'Don't forget to mention Richard may be going to Yale if he gets his cap in Trinity this year.'

'I am very proud of my son just as my father was when I graduated from Trinity. If a man can apply himself to his studies and stick to his guns he'll succeed in his lifetime. Cedric has done this just as I did all those years ago and I am indeed a proud man today.' As he speaks he moves felt-footed to the door; or is it more a lecture than a speech? 'A little cold meat in the larder will be suitable with some of Dowdall's excellent Gentleman's Relish.'

But Mother, lost again in her wistful thoughts of Richard and his achievements, has retrieved from her hold-all a much-read letter from her beloved son. It is just now that Theresa enters to tell her that Jess wishes to see her.

She adds that Jess is expecting Father Conlon at nine o'clock.

'I won't have it. The master and I have decided to knock this nonsense out of her once and for all. I'll speak to Father

Conlon myself. I have no wish, Theresa dear, to speak harshly of your religion but I do think it is not at all suitable for one in Jess's state of health to be got at by the priests. Oh, and by the way, Cedric has got a double first. His father is most satisfied, as I am too, naturally. There's a pencilled note at the bottom of the letter and I'm afraid I can't quite see to read it.'

Theresa obliges by bending over Mother and reading. 'Oh it's for me, Mrs Stewart. Simply "give my love to Theresa".'

'Oh.' Mother folds the letter and puts it into the bag.

Jess's face, yellow-white against the dead white pillowcase. Mother cast-iron in the doorway: 'There you are, Jess dear,' as if Jess could, at this state of her pillaging disease, be anywhere else.

'Well Mother,' always the childhood sniff, apology? No, a forlorn but patiently explaining sniff. 'I hoped you'd manage to get up to see me before Father Conlon comes.'

'I realise that you are nearly of age and that legally I will soon not be able to interfere with your actions but for reasons of allegiance to your family and to all the sacrifices ... '

'What sacrifices, Mother?'

'When your father and I sent you to Switzerland ... '

'Did you and Father have to do without while I was at Davos?'

'We had to curb our expenditures on Maria and the boys' allowance.'

'Did they complain?'

'No. But it was unfortunate for Richard who was having such a wonderful time at Trinity and found it difficult to pay back the hospitality offered him by the other students. He is so popular, you know.'

'I'm sorry about that, Mother. Why didn't you tell me that before?'

'You are deliberately diverting me from my original intention which was to make a firm plea.'

'Well, make it then.'

'Give up the conversion. For your father's sake.'

'I would prefer to discuss that with Father. State your own arguments "against" as clearly as possible.' A fit of coughing sends Mother into a panic and she rings for Theresa who comes at once and holds Jess against her, the spittoon in her left hand under Jess's chin. When a little coloured phlegm comes up at last, Jess subsides, limp, wrecked in body but her mind secured at the moment in its angry loop.

'My reasons are of the purest. You have been carefully reared in the Protestant faith as have my family before me and your father's family before he was born. I should like to add furthermore that as a family we have been considered lenient in the eyes of some of our Protestant neighbours. You may recollect when you were small you were allowed to play ball and walk the dog on Sunday mornings whereas the Walkers and the Bissetts were kept in to sing hymns.'

'Yes, Mother. We were grateful for all that. But I'd like to say that all that has nothing whatsoever to do with my personal religious life.'

'Well, why are you doing it? To hurt us?'

'No, Mother. I have no desire whatsoever to hurt any of the family. In spite of everything I'm fond of you and Pa. Very fond. The reason I asked you to come up this morning was to make my peace with you. If this is not possible then I'd rather you left.'

'I've never heard of such a thing. No one talks to her mother like this.' The age-old phrase comes spitting out of Mother's mouth. 'I was brought up to obey my parents. I simply don't understand the younger generation.' Jess sniffs herself into a smile. 'Cedric has just announced, simply announced in his letter, that he'll be stopping in London for a while. Nobody thinks of their parents any more.'

'Cedric is twenty-two, Mother. And I shall be eighteen

next year. But surely a person's faith is an entirely private affair. I couldn't dream of trying to convert you.'

Now the windy smile becomes a cynical grin which is quickly overlaid by a frown of sympathy for her mother whom she now sees to be stuck in this nervous pretentious groove, unloved, unloving. Well not quite, Jess said afterwards to Theresa when discussing it; there was always Richard.

Perhaps Mother, in spite of the strings she feels loosening all around her, genuinely fears that an unhealthy morbidity has overcome Jess. I often thought that later when going over it in my mind. A woman of little imagination, it's true, but still it surprised me that she should fall into those dreadful cliché stagnancies. Perhaps the rest of the conversation is worth recording, however. Mother went on to say, or rather ask, what brought it on, as though discussing a cold in the head; she also asked whether she or Father had been to blame, remiss in some way, had not guided their daughter carefully enough down the wooden aisles of the Protestant faith. And Jess became patient then. Knowing perhaps that there would be few other opportunities to have it out once and for all. That never again could she, in her physically weakened state, face another row with her mother. What was to be done she wanted done then and there. Otherwise an aching chasm would lie between herself and her parents for the rest of her life.

She attempted a final explanation. 'After my year in Davos I realised that I should never recover from TB. I was almost worse when I returned, you know that. I had always wanted an active life with plenty of interesting things to do. It was most depressing when I realised that I should never do anything satisfying ever again. TB *is* a very depressing disease and unless it can be cured in the earlier stages it has a deteriorating effect on the character. The Catholic Church, however, enshrining as it does the true Christian teaching in all its fullness, has much to offer to those who are helpless and suffering. If I am being verbose, I'm sorry, but I must explain in order to alleviate your horror, disgust almost, at what I intend to do. But my verbosity must verge on the oversimple, most human, if you like, so as you and Pa will realise that I have no desire, whatever, to upset either of you or change your own outlook.'

If Mother interrupted here it would have been merely to repeat what was said earlier. She must, however, have listened to Jess to the end because Jess went on to say that in Father Conlon she had found a relaxation that she never found in any of the Protestant clergymen. She told Mother also that her 'search' had been going on for years – since she was ten, in fact – and that she had always been grateful to Pa who had been generous in giving her the money for all the books she needed, ending on a grumpy note. Jess always tended to be grumpy, although it may seem harsh to judge her for it considering her awful life.

She said then, 'Do you realise I've been stuck in this room now looking over that confounded sea for the last six months; surely you don't grudge me my private needs?'

'Very well,' Mother said, 'I will not interfere with you any further but I cannot guarantee what your father will do.'

'Do, do, do,' Jess shouts, trying to lift herself up on the pillows the better to meet her mother full face. 'What can he do except accept the matter and allow me to live the rest of my life in peace? I've never spoken to you like this before. Indeed, I find it extremely difficult to talk to either you or Father. Maria and Richard seem to be the only two who can communicate with you. You have cut yourself off, Mother, from reality all your life.' Mother, overcome, calls Theresa now, but as Theresa enters Jess puts the last thrust into Mother's breast.

'I don't intend to turn this conversation into a venomous attack. I wish to be alone now. As usual we are at odds with each other. Your own background and upbringing have ruined you. How can you unbend? When the Protestant faith in which you believe so tenaciously tells us repeatedly about a black and unforgiving God?'

'We never looked on it like that.'

'Protestants believe in Christ as a part of history, Catholics as a positive and living figure in their midst. Once you begin to grasp the mystery of transubstantiation then God has broken into the very heart of nature. Try, Mother, to stop worrying about me.'

Mother has no more answers to her daughter's intractability. Theresa, who stands now, unwilling witness to this row, offers a smile of sympathy to Mrs Stewart while feeling pleased for the sake of the invalid that Jess has had the final say. Theresa, perhaps, knew my mother better than any of us after all. Yes, even better than Richard did. Richard in his supreme arrogance merely used his mother's devotion for his own ends, for aggrandising his ego on his varied achievements in the sporting and medical field. Whereas, Maria, poor Maria, disgruntled, puritanical Maria, I don't believe ever trusted Mother completely. Certainly she had a relationship with Pa and for this I am thankful.

My two unhappy sisters!

Jess, however, is somewhat exhilirated now. Theresa who busies herself tidying and preparing for Cedric's return spends many happy hours with Jess.

The following day, while Jess gives her a blow by blow account of her and her mother's contretemps the previous evening – not that Theresa hadn't witnessed the major part – asks Theresa what she's up to.

'I'm doing out Cedric's room.'

'Theresa, you are a laugh. Cedric won't be home for weeks. I have had a *crise de conscience* since our quarrel yesterday. I think perhaps it would have been better if we had accepted our differences silently. I hate upsetting the old people.'

'It's hard to explain things to them, all right. Are you tired? Do you want to be left alone?'

'Not at all. I feel quite cheerful. Sit down and chat. If you have time. I really envy born Catholics who don't have to think – just accept or not, as the case may be.'

'I'm afraid I'm not very pious myself. So I can't help you much.'

'But Theresa, that's wonderful. I don't have to talk about dogma to you.'

'I don't know. It's not that great – our priests can be very nasty.'

'I don't expect them all to be saints! So your hero will be home soon. What surprises are you planning for him? He's not too old for cakes and caresses!'

'Now, now!'

'I'm growing up at last!'

Yes, it's just possible that Jess achieved some small maturity in her lifetime. I know she had one friend, a young man who died in the sanatorium she was in, and there was a glint of happiness between them, I understand, for the short time they were friends. However, I'm sure she had no notion of what was to pass between me and Theresa years after her death.

Theresa says to this barb, 'Well, he'll need his old flannels laundered and his walking shoes mended.'

'It's time he did some of those things for himself.'

'No doubt his new American lady friend will take over one day.'

'Men shouldn't be waited on hand and foot, you know. She'll have a terrible time if you spoil him when he gets home.'

Jess then goes on to say that she has had a letter from James.

'Funny his running away from school like that. He's very brave. Imagine any of the others just getting on ship as cook's assistant and telling them to "drive". That's what he did. Just said "drive". He'd no idea where the ship was going. And didn't care so long as it was going *away*.'

She gives Theresa the letter to read.

I don't think I've ever described Theresa. As a young woman she was very thin, with pale straight hair (light mouse it used to be called), small features. Yes, what you might call a 'petite' young woman. She had a catchy voice, one of her most endearing attributes, which always seemed on the rim of laughter although she seldom laughed out loud. She always dressed plainly – cotton dresses and starched white collars and she smelled of cotton. Her lovely sallow skin used to shine like polished bone when she was happy. What else can I say about her? Her supreme intelligence which others often bitchily said was a spin-off from her association with us. I deny this, however. That she came as a nursemaid, only half-educated, was not uncommon in those days. In the twenties anyone was glad to get a job, even as a kitchen maid, in the house of a professional man like my father. No, her intelligence was native to her. I think she was far more intelligent than any of us. She had an uncanny way of knowing how things would go but never trying to interfere with what she felt was the inevitable. And her sensitivity towards everyone in the house was a phenomenon we all shared. That is not to say that she was weak or hypocritical. On the contrary. She simply had an unending supply of sympathy for those in any way needful of it. However, to go back to the letter.

Dear Jess,

Very pretty landscapes and the people are friendly too. I have a temporary job in a hotel. Sort of bell-boy. Forgive this short note but I think of you and hope you are out and about. June is the only bearable month in Ireland as I remember it.

Theresa interrupts her reading with, 'You'd think he'd been gone half a lifetime.'

I am boarding with a family called Whadish, there are four boys ranging in ages from four to fourteen and two daughters, one of whom is learning English from me. My regards to Father and Mother (if they want to have them).

Your affectionate brother,

James.

Theresa smiles, 'He does say a lot all the same.'

'About the young lady to whom he's teaching English? It did cross my mind. Wouldn't it be wonderful if one of us were happy in the end?'

'Well, Richard's all right. He'll get what he wants. He'll be a successful doctor and husband. He'll marry an Irish girl and settle down comfortably in Blackrock or somewhere.'

'You do make it sound dull.'

'What's dull about contentment?'

'You're too clever by half, Theresa. Where did we find you?'

'Under a cabbage like the rest of you.'

'Do you know that I used actually to try and find the cabbage when I was little. I remember the one I chose. A rather handsome York down at the end of the hill garden.'

The door opens and Maria enters, dressed in riding clothes. She, all bustle and worry, is at the mercy as usual of her freedom. A strange paradox. She was free because she was unfree. She had no choice. Her life was a blueprint of the horsey girl who turns into a horsey woman. I think I said earlier that she might have been a suffragette if she had been born a little sooner. But as it was, her mind was padlocked behind generations of stiff Protestant notions, prim as a governess yet she never would even achieve that status. She 'disapproved' of everything. She would spend her life waiting from Monday to Thursday for the weekly meet of the Bray Harriers. During the weekend she read what we used to slay as middle-brow books, but the romance in them, or rather the effect of the romance in them, was something she hid within herself. I pitied her more than Jess. Especially afterwards when I discovered she had secretly painted stacks of water-colours, mostly views of the bay, which were tinted with nostalgia that would break your heart were you to see them today. So why could she not share any of this agony with the rest of us? For the same reason, I suppose, that we were all cut off from each other; like points in a field, I think I said before.

Now when Jess teases her about the cabbage mystery Maria insists that 'It all sounds very silly to me.'

'Of course it's silly. But it wasn't then. A matter of grave importance.'

'What time is the meet?' Theresa, now, conscious that a change of subject might be wise.

'It's at half past ten. I can't think where Pa has got to. We have to be at the livery stables half an hour before to hack over to Calary. The meet's near Jim's farm.'

This was Jim Magee, the well-known horse-coper.

She fusses out on this note and Jess and Theresa exchange a ripple of laughter.

'Well, where were we? Oh yes. Cedric. Never very far from brother Cedric.'

'Do you think they will marry?'

'It would seem so. She sounds an exciting lady,' Jess says.

'Has he lost all sense? At his age. How can he know what he wants?'

'Theresa!'

'Well he has. How does he know she'll travel? His

whole ambition is to go east. And those Americans put their comfort above everything.'

'But America's a great country. Look at all we've gained from America.'

'Gosh and Golly. And OK and Robert Taylor and Greer Garson. Most of the film stars anyway are foreign. Greta Garbo, Anna Mae Wong, Marlene Dietrich. Leslie Howard is English.'

'Theresa! What's got into you. I never heard you run down Americans before. You love the pictures. I've never known you miss a Thursday night at Ballybrack.'

'I'm not going any more. It's too chilly.'

'Really! Because of Cedric's impending engagement you've even taken against the village hall. That's amazing.'

You think I'm making up this conversation, which in a way is true. But from what Jess told me afterwards, Theresa's reaction to my impending marriage was more than a little emphatic. Please do not believe I was light-hearted with rapture at the prospect myself. Oxford, for me, had a density of human approach which I found difficult to assimilate. As I said, I never wanted to join anything but often found myself dragged here or there out of curiosity to listen to someone who might supplement my ideas, both political and sociological, at the time. It was here I met my future wife. I found her refreshing in her lack of acceptance of a norm so coveted by her English contemporaries, who in spite of their seeking a common ground on the left were unable to shake off the shackles of their forbears, who maintained a fiercely conservative outlook on everything non-political. On the other hand I found her depressingly logical, materialistic, and I missed what might be termed as an Irish attribute (or might have been then before our own country became a materialistic miasma with the rise of its new bourgeoisie), an ability to ride on intuition. Was I in love? Sufficient for now to say that I was infatuated with her sexually. Her delightfully clean-curved body was an obsession that was with me night and day. When, finally, we slept together I was what would nowadays be called hooked. The fact that when she became pregnant I was already beginning to tire of her is something that will be dealt with later during this narrative.

But as I have said, this is not strictly speaking the story of Cedric, it is merely what flashes in and out of my memory, of the events that happened in this house, on whose paint-peeling stairs I sit now – what a house and a family does to everyone, how lives are shaped and generations shoved into each other like the bellows of a concertina.

It was three weeks later that I returned to the hearth: debonair, oh yes, full of my extraordinary academic achieve-ments and ready to crush my less brilliant brothers and sisters like a stone crushing an egg if any of them tried to get the better of me. It must be remembered, too, that it was 1939 and the war was imminent so for other reasons I was glad to get to Ireland for a breather from the hysteria on the other side of the Irish Sea. My fiancée had gone to the States for her vacation.

Cedric, living now at the point of beautiful change, comes bounding up the last few yards of Kilmore hill. A young man in corduroys, tweed jacket and open-necked shirt. He has a mat of black hair which he likes to let grow down the nape and those almost purple eyes that were undeniably the best feature of the Stewart family. It is Maria whom he meets first as he utters the familiar, 'I'm home! Where's everyone?'

Maria, in her low, almost whining voice, says, 'Ma's at the wireless. Listening to the news.'

She does not reach up to him as he pecks her on the cheek, but the lovely weather, the sweep of grass, the insects grappling with their life cycles invade him with a feeling of heavenly contentment which his words 'There'll be a war' do nothing to mar. 'It can't be avoided now. If Germany invades Poland, that'll be it. What is called the rights of small nations will be used as the excuse. We are told we must fight for this.'

He sits himself comfortably on the grass beside her and pulls a piece of long grass out of its sheaf ignoring the squeak it makes as he begins to suck.

'What do you mean "we"?' Maria asks, two lines over the nose brindled in the sunshine.

'Well, not necessarily Ireland. But we are a small nation.'

'What will happen here?'

'De Valera will keep our neutrality.'

'How do you know?'

'Strategically we're not much use to England. Unless America comes in.' He lies back and watches the fleecy clouds tearing about like white feathers from a swan. 'I suppose Ma told you I'm going to marry a Boston lady.'

'Not a very good time to get married.'

'People don't stop getting married just because of the war. Rather the opposite I should think. Dear old Blighty and all that.'

'You're not thinking of joining up?'

'When I was in London – don't tell Ma or Pa yet – I had an interview with a daily as a correspondent. If I get the job, and if the war can't be prevented, I suppose I'll be sent off with the army somewhere.'

'Will it be like the last war?'

'This war will be fought in the air. It will be over in a few weeks.'

'You can't know.'

'Everybody in England thinks Germany can't possibly stand up to the British airforce. There'll be France and the Netherlands on their side as well.'

'Mussolini will back Hitler. We'll all be killed.'

Cedric, feeling his level of tolerance recede, begins a long resigned sigh which is interrupted by the raising of a voice from the drawing room. His sister's gloomy thoughts have already begun to infect him, dampen his high spirits, and these obvious snarls coming from the drawing room augment the malaise which he feels is all too quickly descending on him.

'Cheer up,' he attempts to his sister as he rises from the grass, 'I bet you'll be sitting on this very lawn this time next year wondering why you had this conversation. How's your mare?'

'She's lame.'

So that was it – not the war, not the inconclusiveness of her life. Her horse was lame and she was thrown into a pit of despondency.

It may not have been like that at all. But as we grew up and saw each other less and less frequently we all tended to assume the others hadn't changed. But for all I knew Maria was probably going through an awful crisis. She was about twenty-five then, I suppose, and with little hope of ever breaking away or asserting herself as an individual. Jess, strangely enough, imprisoned as she was in her bed had much more internal freedom than Maria would ever achieve. So as Cedric rises now he is only half aware of his sister's inner torment.

In the drawing room the curtains are half-drawn and dimly he perceives his mother framed by the back of the grandfather chair, very erect, very blunt of feature. She stretches up to his formal peck at the hairline. 'There you are, Cedric dear, sit down quietly.' The wireless drones on with its mouthings of doom. 'Do you think Richard will join up?'

'Why on earth should he? He hasn't done his finals yet at

Trinity. He's Irish. Much more Irish than I am.'

'De Valera will not hold back.'

'For heaven's sake. Dev wasn't Secretary of the United Nations for nothing. We're no use to England.'

'What about our ports?'

'For one thing, the war will be in Europe. Be sensible. What good would our ports be in that event? Can we forget the war for a minute? I was hoping that everyone in Ireland would be just living their own lives. I was so pleased to be on the mail boat. Dún Laoghaire was beautiful this morning as the sun was rising.'

'Jess has finally turned.'

'Well done she!'

'How can you say that?' Mother, shocked into standing up, shocked even into switching off the wireless, turns on her son but he drags from somewhere some frail strength. 'She has established herself at last as an individual. Instead of just being a bundle of sick flesh.'

'Cedric, you don't know what you're talking about. You're far too young to understand the effect this sort of thing has on people's parents.'

'I can't understand what the parents have to do with it. And I am twenty-two.' Aware that his fist, tightly balled up, has been pressing the marble chimneypiece so hard that it has begun to hurt, he tries to ease his limbs out of their tautness by blurting, 'Thank you and Pa for your letter.'

'I hope that since you have been so successful in your studies you won't let your achievements go to waste.'

'No, Mother.' And after a pause, 'You are well, I hope.'

'I have not been well at all.'

'I trust nothing serious?'

'All this worry about Jess has taken its toll. On your father as well.'

A few more moments of uncertain hovering he knows are all he'll be able to stand. Perhaps a murmur of commiseration or an offer of advice not to dwell so much on something which is now out of her hands and he is gone from the room, his breath coming hot and sporadic. He knows if he doesn't see Theresa or Jess soon something will snap. In the kitchen Ellie gives him a fat welcome, slobbering and winsome as ever, but to his plea of 'Where's Theresa?' she bursts out laughing. 'God, you bitch,' he wants to shout but doesn't, leaves quickly and hurls through the back door into the kitchen garden. All the old smells: parsley, mint and that fresh-dug earth smell, the sun hot on his shoulders, the sea below shining like amethyst and Theresa, at last, picking raspberries into a punnet already stained in pink and purple.

He pouts, 'You weren't on the steps to welcome me.' Kisses, but only her ear, holding the thin-boned shoulder in his fist. He takes a handful of raspberries from the punnet.

'You can pick your own.' She can't but smile at the impudence. 'Anyway, I didn't want to interfere with your mother's.'

'Since when did Mother welcome me home? When I walked into the drawing room she told me to shut up. I don't give a tuppenny God's curse. It's you I've come home to see.'

'I hope you'll cheer us up. The place is like a morgue. Your mother and father glued to the wireless when they're not tormenting Jess.'

'You haven't even kissed me.'

Theresa straightens one of the canes that has been bent by some animal or other. 'That Towser is forever amongst the fruit.'

'Well?' he makes his lips into a circle.

'You're too tall.' And she hurries down the row of raspberries, snatching the odd fruit here and there.

He feels transparent left standing like that, or even invisible, till he runs after her and catches her sleeve. 'You don't seem to care whether I'm home or not. You're worse than Maria. She … all she cares about is whether the war will stop her hunting. And all Mother … '

'That's enough. I never knew such a family for backbiting.'

'Well, say something. Or I will. I want your blessing.'

'You have it without asking. Is she pretty?'

Cedric presents a somewhat blurred photo of himself and his fiancée. Theresa takes it in her hard little hand and looks into it as though the girl were beside her to be vetted, criticised, torn apart, but instead of loyalty towards the woman he has chosen to marry he only feels puzzled by his need for Theresa to approve. She must, he feels, like her. All seems, just now, to rest on this. But, 'It's not very good of you,' is all she says as she hands back the snap with a brief smile.

'Is that all?'

'No, she's lovely. And I wish you happiness if happiness is possible.'

'You're far too sophisticated. She wants the wedding soon on account of the war.'

'The war hasn't broken out yet.' She has now nearly filled her punnet with Cedric's help, who has fallen gratefully into the old ways, taking pleasure in finding the fattest raspberries – like milking a tiny cow, he used to say – so as to fill up the punnet more quickly. 'That'll do,' she says, asking quickly will he get married in Ireland. No, he won't, he tells her. With American parents, a quick hitch, as she puts it, in a Chelsea registry office.

'That'll give your parents something to talk about.'

They walk now along the weedy paths, he with his arm about her shoulders, which move like two little animals independently from the rest of her body. They speak of Jess and Cedric says how happy he is for her.

CHAPTER SEVENTEEN

I THINK IT WAS THEN THAT THERESA recounted what had gone on between Mother and Jess before her final conversion, explaining how Jess had stuck to her guns in spite of everything. I knew then, in no religious sense, that one of us was saved. Saved from being the eternal yes-man, something, in spite of my own iron will, I've had to fight against all my life.

Before they reach the back door he cries out as though from some distant time, 'For God's sake, kiss me, or I'll go away and never come back.'

He takes her up then in his arms like a lover, he thinks, but she, Theresa, doesn't think this because her kiss is firm, formal and as she turns her head she asks, 'Is she in the family way?'

'Yes.'

'Then you must marry her.'

He hadn't meant to tell, or bring the pregnancy up to anyone. Just marry, get it over with, for he knows now he doesn't love or want to love her, only do the damn dutiful thing that he must. His own fault because of skin and thighs – oh and a little intellectual rapport, receding now that plans have been so bluntly constructed: her parents arriving from the States, Mr and Mrs Every American, lawyers both; no give there, he imagines. But that Theresa has so quickly assessed the situation he is now glad. Because secrets from each other would be unbearable at this moment.

He smells roast lamb as the back door opens. The cream is cooling in the dairy beside the scullery. The wide churn into which the milk is poured each morning allows the cream to be easily skimmed from the top. He thinks of the raspberries and how they will follow the lamb, the roast potatoes and peas and how the cream will lighten the colour of the fruit before he tastes it. He hasn't eaten like this for many moons and won't again either. For a short minute he envies Richard's single-mindedness, to stay at home and get on with it like his father and his grandfather, a doctor too, did also. But no, it is not for him, he knows, to dangle his toes in the Irish stream of his Stewart forbears, nor follow any of the obvious professions – doctor, lawyer – still more or less Protestant strongholds although the wind of change is beginning to ruffle the branches of their Church's ascendancy.

Speeches from the wireless resounding in the corridor – Mother again with the volume full – he climbs, now reluctantly, to Jess's room. The sun aslant the bedclothes touching the pillow accentuates a face, a cross face, sickly, almost putty-coloured against the blaze of the pillowcase. Books are everywhere, crushing the eiderdown, some fallen half-open on the floor, but the eyes are not following any print; they stare at the ceiling.

'Jess!'

She lets her pupils travel to his and a wet smile opens the dead face for a moment. 'You've been here a long time,' she says accusingly.

'I know, I know. I spoke of you – to Mother, to Theresa. Congratulations. Tough little girl.'

She laughs horribly. 'Damn it. I'm too tough to eat! I'm stone,' she continues relentlessly, 'dying.'

'No, no,' he wants to scream. His double first, his

impending marriage, his kiss or non-kiss with Theresa, the possibility of his becoming a journalist with the best left-wing … oh hell, all thrown in the dirt before this small dying animal spread underneath the bedclothes, his youngest sister, the youngest of the family.

'Calm down,' he says, surprising himself. 'You are not dead yet. At least help me to unscatter my emotions.'

'All right,' the smile is almost unspiteful now, 'tell again about the beauties of Dún Laoghaire in the early morning, the pastoral scenes at Oxford, your young lady – should I congratulate you?'

'You want to hear how the English expect the Irish to make jokes all the time? Speak with what they call a brogue? So we pretend. Or be bored secretly. Why I'm marrying an American perhaps, although Americans too pall with their hundred per cent materialism polished and shining with pseudo-romanticism. Yes, not sex after all; romantic "I love you" stuff.'

'Worse than the Irish,' Jess suddenly laughs freely for once.

'And as soon as they get you they have the all-American parents on the next boat to witness your signature. Oh gee, oh gosh.'

'Do they not want to see Ireland first?' Jess, displaying now her teeth, darkened by the damage of her disease. 'All Americans imagine Ireland full of bogs and pigs and so, so quaint.'

'The English worse sometimes.'

'Why stay?'

'How did you guess?'

'Well you're not going to stay here? Surely.' Spitefully again she glares around her room, her island in the midst of the buffoonery of Protestantism, outdating briskly but clinging to distant snobberies of all kinds. 'And the war will make it difficult for you. You could be called up if they have conscription.'

'Which of course they will.'

'So then?'

'Ah-ha, I've foreseen that already; I've a job, I think.'

'Intelligence?'

'No, better, hopefully. To see and not be seen by the enemy.'

'And no war yet,' she laughs. 'May yet be postponed.'

'I doubt it.'

'So do I. So you're a cub reporter?'

'All right, love. Tell me. Blow by blow.'

So Jess told then, of the long uphill struggle with the parents. How it took its toll physically on her dwindling health but how she knew she'd wrested some sort of logic from within her consciousness and it, if nothing else, filled up the void with which she had lived since she became ill.

He wants to ask her why he is alive, since once he is at home he finds nothing to live for. Once he had thought his lady friend a good reason for continuing but it's only when he is away from here that he feels cut out for intelligence, beauty, some as yet unimagined heights. When he's home it's the same old emotional void, the feeling of only being the odd man out in the family. And yet again that's not even true, because James was in the same boat, even further out than he. But he, James, is now truly out of sight – lucky man. Yet ... in spite of his awful depressions which sometimes follow each other like waves on to a beach, in the end he is glad to be himself and himself alone. Aren't we all – oh cynicism – narcissistic to the bone, he thinks; even his dying sister there under her guilt, her books, her Roman Catholicism?

Looking back on Cedric I realise he was a great soul-searcher and arrogant with it. But the soul-searching didn't last all that long – not much after his thirties, that is – because by then he had begun to accumulate money by devious ways, mostly thievery in a moribund empire. Oh yes, he is well known now as an expert in Chinese, Burmese; his house in Chelsea is like a museum where experts go to compare notes and back-slap. Yes, while I sit on this stair I say this with no pride whatsoever. What I am to this house and this house is to me is the only important thing left while my father dies obtrusively in the drawing room.

But there they were, Jess and Cedric, glaring not un-affectionately at each other, both having grown up in each other's absence, with a whole file of brand new thoughts and conceptions to trade with each other. This may be an interesting holiday after all, Cedric begins to think.

'Mother is worried that Richard will be filled with false fervour and rush to England to join the Medical Corps or something.'

'Pa is worried about you,' she counters.

'He is?' Cedric chews this over. 'He probably thinks I'm too young to get married and he's probably right.'

'So you've got her pregnant.'

'Oh my God.' Cedric groans loudly, mockingly. 'So you and Theresa decided already that my girlfriend is pregnant, you two little bitches, gossipy little … '

'Cedric! You know that Theresa and I never gossip. If we both have arrived at this most obvious fact it's individually and alone. And that's not what Pa is worried about. He worries that you'll be carried away, seeing as you are more English than the rest of us.'

'So I'm the eccentric Irishman in England, English in Ireland. No wonder …

'Anyway, I've no intention of fighting for someone else's king, whatever the family may think that I've become an Englishman because of the influence of my education. It goes the other way if anything. Over there I'm more Irish than here. Anyway I'll meet him at the station and get the first encounter over with as quickly as possible.'

Cedric is called for lunch then and he bends to kiss his sister whose face quilts up expectantly under the caress. As he leaves the room she asks him will he exchange rooms with her. Secretly. She cannot stand the view any longer. All in terror – for it is Pa who insists that Jess be made more cheerful by the sight of the beautiful bay – he agrees as he takes the stairs in a bundle of animal appetite, the lamb again wafting up through the house. It is home: silver, mahogany, lace mats, wine in the decanter, Mother complaining about everything. Yes, home all right.

So Cedric and Jess exchange rooms, not without a certain amount of childish giggling. Had antibiotics been discovered in the early thirties when Jess was only incubating the disease she would undoubtedly have lived to quite an age but as it was the disease had gone too far and even though she didn't die then, lived three more years in fact, her emaciated physique had lost its power of recovery. But now with the laughter that shakes them both as he carries her feather-light body into his newly made bed she feels a renewed will to remain cheerful, positive, and relive what she can or rather live how she can during Cedric's brief stay in Ireland. They chatter about their bedroom gods.

'Shall I keep the Bosch? I like it.'

Torn from a German art magazine and framed in front of a dim old seascape print of Mother's, Cedric offers it willingly. Tells her he has more prints to unpack now, speaks of Braque, Picasso, and she wants an early Picasso, delicate; crossly saying she doesn't like cubism, an experiment, she says, which takes from life in a way the impressionists didn't. She, now dwarfed in his larger bed, watches him as he journeys to and fro with her books, cups, bottles, muttering that he's given up the Church completely but couldn't embark on another facet of Christianity like she has. Complaining that she is an intellectual whereas he, the romantic, could not possibly absorb all those facts into his system.

Jess sniffs: 'Digging for compliments!'

'No, no. On the contrary. A double first doesn't necessarily mean an extra-inquisitive mind. Quite the contrary I sometimes think!'

'Rot!' she says. 'You're just OK without a God!' remembering, too late, Theresa's veto on Americanisms since Cedric's engagement. In fact she tells him a little now of Theresa's reaction which Cedric interprets as generosity on her part. But later, in the kitchen, over a long tea and chat he looks at her from time to time uneasily.

Now, still busy with Jess he offers her a cowrie, a large one, as a present from his marine collection. 'You can hear the sea in this so if Pa complains you can say you've exchanged sight for sound.' She holds the shell in such a way that he becomes embarrassed by its sexuality, wants to take it back. But she shrugs under the blankets.

'Leave it there,' she says, vague.

He is restless now, wanting to be off for perhaps further chat with Theresa before it's time to meet his father's train, but she holds him there with 'I've stolen your view of the McDonnell household.'

It is conceivable that Cedric had quite forgotten Carmel; his efforts at the disentanglement of his present thoughts send his mind galloping back to that now somewhat shameful afternoon in her bedroom, the girl crying senselessly over her first infatuation, himself: well, gutted might be an apt description of his post-non-coital condition! He wants to laugh now that it's so far safely behind him. Till he thinks of the weeks ahead and why not? Jess tells him she's working as a secretary.

'Oh, what a fall is … ' Cedric laughs. 'From potential film star to typist.'

'She had an offer, I believe, from Hollywood but her father persuaded her not to think about it.'

'So much for Catholic leniency. *Plus ça change*, etcetera.'

'Perhaps the war clouds.'

'Perhaps.'

'Why don't you stay in Ireland?'

Cedric looks down at his sister, looking just now not more than twelve years old as when he used to push her, all wrapped in rugs, on the swing under the chestnut tree. And how quickly she used to tire and say in cross pouting tones, 'Let me down.' So now he was letting her down on her deathbed by his insistence on making England his future. England, that is, if much further away weren't possible.

'It's very stuffy in here,' she says since he doesn't reply and Cedric throws up the window. The McDonnell house sleepy in the sunshine shows no sign of life – very different from those long ago days, that summer before he went up to Oxford.

CHAPTER EIGHTEEN

WHAT HAD HAPPENED TO CEDRIC during those four previous years? Surely he came back and forth during the holidays. Yes he did of course and once in a while saw Carmel. But so busy was he with his change of lifestyle that his visits home were lived in a cocoon of study. During two of the long summer vacations he travelled in Europe and Egypt and barely lit on Killiney. His thoughts always on the edge of some future stage in his academic career. So this is the first time I remember his taking it all in again so richly. And earlier this year before the June exams: that breakdown, the stomach pumping, the nausea, his unfortunate fiancée believing it was all her fault, following up quickly with his promise to 'try again'.

'Oh why, why?' she kept asking.

'God, it's not your fault,' he had to tell her a hundred times. And it wasn't either. Something in him that he feared might recur any time. The doctors had names for it but were quite unhelpful. Only his snowballing back into his studies brought him through. At least, then, the family and Theresa were ignorant of this. But he feared Theresa would know in her uncanny way. A line let slip in a letter, anything. No, she mustn't know, mustn't find out what might be to her the ultimate betrayal.

CHAPTER NINETEEN

THE OLD STATION IS QUIET this evening, no wind. The station-master's 'Good evening, Mr Stewart' sends him into the present.

'Yes,' he says, shyly.

'Back again?'

'Yes.'

A goods train shrugs through on its way to Dublin and he crosses the line by the metal bridge the better to see the train as it puffs through the little tunnel this side of Killiney hill. Ice clamps around his heart as the familiar singing comes up the lines. His father steps down, straight as a parade sergeant, his briefcase fussing at his side. They shake hands formally.

'You had a good crossing, I hope?'

'It was like a dream. You wouldn't know you were sailing. The boat was crowded, of course.'

His father, a head and neck shorter than he, takes short steps to his long strides as they trace the railway line to the foot of the hill. He stops here and says firmly. 'This will be England's last war.'

'They say it will be over quite soon.'

'We must prepare for the worst. In 1914 we thought it would end by Christmas. Do not forget that your two uncles were killed in that war. Wars are terrible, terrible. You may stay here, Cedric. Everything is open to you now with your fine achievements behind you.'

'But Father … ' How can he tell him that he can't stay? That here he will suffocate.

'I do not wish to lose any of my family. But I have lost Jess.'

'She may get better, Father.'

They climb the hill, silently open the little gate at the bottom of the kitchen garden. The rows of cabbages are yellow from lack of rain. As they reach the tennis court the father stops again. 'I'll get Barton to cut the grass so as we can knock a ball about tonight.'

'But Father, I'm not in favour of war. Honestly.' Honestly? Is there not that frisson of excitement stirring in his chest at this very moment?

'It is only those who sit around doing nothing who welcome change,' his father says.

'I want change, Father. A better deal for the less well-off. And for me travel is my main desire. I've read history at Oxford, Father. But what do I know of the world?' The very stiffness of his own words is beginning to strangle. But he must hear his father out, the man to whom he owes so much and to whom he can give nothing back.

'If the war comes, and I don't see how it can be avoided, you may have to postpone your idea of "finding out" by getting to know yourself better.' The dog suddenly rushes down the bank to welcome Pa, mad as a derailed train he twirls and leaps, rolls over and over. His father bends and automatically fondles the animal, touching lovingly the fur while Cedric stands scorched in his own embarrassment.

'Forgive my clumsiness. May we speak later?'

'I'm a little bit done in. You must do what you think best. I myself did not volunteer for the last war. I put my family before everything.'

'Yes, Father. Yes. You may be sure I'll let you know before I make my decisions.' That he gets this out even is a tremendous relief. Now he can shake himself away, he feels, without doing or being done any further damage.

So they gather, inevitably, for the evening meal. More formal than lunch, candles glitter in the three-pronged silver candlestick. Wine swims rose red in the decanters. Theresa prepares Jess's tray on the sideboard while Father carves the cold meat left over from lunch. A large heaped salad stands in the Waterford glass bowl; there is mint sauce and redcurrant jelly in small silver jugs. Maria sits beside Cedric, her long bony fingers playing with her as yet unused fork. She says, her voice dark in the dark of the room, 'I got the vet for Nessa. Jim rang me and said the fetlock was still very swollen.'

'Perhaps you should get her fired. Plenty of horses hunt with fired legs.'

'I'd prefer a mild blister. I can never sell a fired mare.'

'Do you plan to sell her? That's a surprise.'

'Well,' she plays with the fork more nervously, 'Jim has a young cob, a six-year-old belonging to Mrs De Burgh in Greystones who hunted all last season. A chestnut, quite stylish. Do you recall, Father? An honest sort of animal, Jim says.'

'Mrs De Burgh's a crook!' Father laughs roundly and Maria goes white. 'A couple of months more on grass will probably see the end of the trouble anyway. Don't fret, pet.'

'But the cubbing starts early September.'

'You may borrow my horse Slaney if you wish. I won't have time to go cubbing this autumn. There are a lot of cases listed.'

Cedric sighs silently, hoping now that Maria will relax – the played fork is driving into his skull.

'That's very kind of you, Father. Perhaps I could bring him in at the end of August and hack him out every day to get used to him.'

'Isn't that rather an expense, dear?' Mother cuts in, having comfortably surrounded herself with food dishes.

Maria looks from one parent to another and Cedric dreads a prolonged scene. But Father abruptly changes the subject, addressing Cedric. 'Have you tried the wine?'

Cedric picks up his glass. 'A nice Bordeaux at a guess.' He holds it sideways. 'Did   you get it for some special reason?' But his father is busy carving second helpings and does not – or pretends not to – hear.

'Do you not think it's time that Theresa ate with us? Especially now that Ellen's about to leave?'

Maria nearly knocks over her glass in amazement, looks daggers in all directions as though calling the gods to witness what she can't believe she's heard.

'So my son's become a left-winger.'

Theresa too swings on Cedric, her tray nearly over-balancing in the process. 'How dare you?' she says, quite white. 'How dare you talk to your parents like that? Especially with me in the room.'

Cedric feels the tears now. He has made a fool of himself as usual. What can he say, do, right in this house? He may never acquit himself as he'd like to. He cannot stay any longer in the dining room but how can he go without causing further scenes? He sticks it out therefore. Letting the desultory talk dribble round him unmindful of its content. He cannot lift his eyes to Theresa, although she has already forgiven him his lack of tact. Yes, simply clumsy, that's all he is. Unforgivably insensitive.

CHAPTER TWENTY

IT BECOMES CLEARER AND CLEARER to me now, as I sit on this top stair that I am not telling a story about wars or family deaths but about love. But this is just my huge difficulty.

CHAPTER TWENTY-ONE

' GOODNIGHT VIENNA, a city of a million memories,
My heart is waiting on the edge of the ... '

Cedric sits in his room that now overlooks the sea when he
hears a strange noise, a gulping sound like the plug being
removed from the bath and the water bolting down the pipe.
He switches off the wireless and pokes out his head, curious
in a vague way about the numerous emotions that he feels
are overtaking or overriding his own ambivalent feelings
towards the rest of the family. But he doesn't expect to see
his father, the cause of this strange noise, sitting (just where
I'm sitting now) on the top stair and weeping – howling
would be a better word. The sobs tear down the staircase. He
is dressed not for the office but for the meet in a green
hunting jacket and the north light casts a silver streak down
the centre of the back. His shoulders are hunched and his
strong grey hair, usually flatly brushed, stands up like wire
wool on his skull. Hesitant as to whether a retreat would be
the lesser of the two evils – that is, mumbling trite sympathies
towards the old man or pretending not to have heard. For
what could be worse, he argues, than for this 'man of iron'
to be caught breaking down in front of his eldest son? And
yet he must tender his hand which he places now as gently
as he can on his father's shoulder.

'What is it, Pa? Is there anything I can do?'

'She is far too young.' Who? Maria? Jess? Dead? Cedric goes cold right down to his ankles; his whole body losing the impetus of moving, he remains fixed, drained of speech.

'The priests have got at her.' God what a relief! It's Jess's conversion as usual. And Cedric's heart is suddenly hardened.

'Not that young. Suffering matures. You must allow her her relaxation in grace. It means so much to her. Supplies something that her own life can't.' He hears the old clichés stumbling after each other but how else communicate his point when these formal speeches are their only interchange?

'May I tell you a story, Father? Do I dare?'

'What is it then?' The sobs, thank heaven, have subsided.

'Very well. But you won't like it.' Cedric feels his pulse racing but he can't stop now. 'When I was about eight or nine I heard something Sally said. Do you remember her, Father? A maid who was with us for only a few months – I think she was sacked for stealing. Anyway I overheard her say something which has stuck in my mind ever since. She said, "Them Prods is all perverts." I wasn't supposed to be listening, or else she thought I was too young to take it in. But the word hung around all day in my head. Pervert? And the venom with which she used the word. Pervert? So we were all perverts? Eventually I looked the word up in the dictionary. Perverse meant obstinately or wilfully wrong, peevish, wicked. And a pervert could mean a person showing sexual deviation. Now remember I was young and quite ignorant of the world. I was overthrown by this definition of all Protestants: we were all wicked, because naturally my child's mind looked on the worst meaning as the maid's interpretation of us all. In truth I was dreadfully upset. So Father, I beg of you now, stop thinking that Jess has fallen into a kind of religious ruin. Stop torturing yourself. Think of her. How she lost her one friend in Davos. A young man with whom she found some emotional rapport and who died cursing God. Perhaps she loved him.'

'Excuse me for having let go.' His father turns his head sideways to the hand which still rests on his shoulder; fearing yet desperately needing some form of caress, Cedric sharply withdraws his hand and it hovers like a hawk just above his father's head.

'You at least have not lost the faith. You still believe?'

What can Cedric say to this pitiful plea?

'Yes, Father, or rather no. I am, I think, an agnostic.'

Anger at last releases the pent-up venom in the old man.

'I scraped every penny I had to give you three a fine start and the girls a proper feeling of puritan good.'

'But Jess, Father? Isn't she different, sick as she is?'

'Don't speak any more about it.' He gets wearily up. 'I'm going hunting with Maria. Call her will you?'

'I don't like to see you upset like this. You've worked too hard all your life. Enjoy your ride now with Maria and you'll feel better this evening.' What other reparation can he make?

'I'm deeply disappointed in you.'

'What can I say?'

'Think about it. For my sake.'

'I have thought about it, Father.'

'You mean you believe in nothing.'

'Not exactly. But I simply cannot, cannot, adhere to any formal teachings of either Church – that is, the two main bodies, the Roman Catholic and the Protestant. So if I believe in Christ, then only as an extension of myself. I must believe in myself if I am to survive as a "Christian" thinker.'

'I abhor selfishness. Only by being selfless can we succeed in this world.'

'What is success, then?'

'If you don't know after your splendid career in Oxford then you will never know.'

'I don't look on exam results as success, Father. Success is only something that happens within oneself. I wish I were a poet, or an artist, then I would know what success or failure was. But I can only be a cipher, a learned one at best.'

'Losing the allegiance of your sons and daughters is failure. I built this family. I planned, long before you were born, to buy this place and call you after my father Cedric. He was a good man. He refused a knighthood from Queen Victoria on the grounds that he believed no one should be knighted for tending the poor. And he never wavered in his faith.'

'Times have changed. The whole of Europe's in turmoil. We mustn't expect everyone to act the same way as they did in your day.'

'The most fearful war was fought in my lifetime.'

What can Cedric say? Either to convince or explain his own dilemma.

'I'll call Maria.' They are both standing now on the top stair, nothing settled between them. Perhaps his father made a better effort than in the foregoing here recorded but his cold determination not to unbend, once having stifled the sobs which made obvious his anguish, certainly left Cedric in a worse void than ever. There was one thing he always regretted afterwards not having said: how much he had appreciated the wine. For he knew that his father had most carefully chosen it for him. But what use is love if it can never be expressed except at one remove?

That's why I said above that the telling of love is my huge difficulty and yet as sure as anything, that is what this book is about.

CHAPTER TWENTY-TWO

THAT SUMMER WORE ON SLOWLY. I didn't get in touch with Carmel – not out of loyalty to my future wife, but because I was upset by my family's lack of trust. I lay often on the grass chewing and reading. I also spent much time in my room grimacing into the mirror. I spent less time than usual also with Theresa. Not intentionally, though. It seemed as though she were avoiding me and when I tried to rectify matters I became dumb, shy, oversensitive to her possible reactions. I did talk to Jess, trying to get to know her before it was too late, and a lot of her fussiness, her irritability, wore off. I flatter myself to say that I may have eased things for her considerably because Pa seemed less inclined to grumble or nag and Mother, involved as she was with Richard's doings, left the rest of us largely alone. Once or twice I carried Jess into the garden to sit in the shade and we exchanged views on every subject under the sun.

My impending marriage was widely discussed and when I got a telegram to say she was arriving, this naturally set the house into turmoil. But the main thing that worried me was that her pregnancy would show and then really I'd have to admit to throwing the cat among the pigeons. How could I explain to her, either, that my parents were a whole generation behind hers in thought and deed. American parents thought, I believed then, exclusively about the personal welfare and happiness of their children whereas we Irish had to put up with those to whom moral fibre was the only attribute worth having. However, she arrived with all her splendid New World trappings: coat hangers and suitcases as large as coffins made of bright yellow pigskin that I secretly considered to be in the worst of taste. My ancient cracked fibre suitcase, battered and strapped, I felt to be a more harmonious adjunct to an Irishman's journeyings. However. Well, I can see it all. The usual amethyst-laden sea in the harbour, the old mail boat grumbling in, subsiding with a heavy sigh by the sea wall. Staunch old vessel much trod by the emigrant Paddy. Yes, there she was – my fiancée, not the boat – gleaming from her recent holiday in the States, expecting me to throw my arms around her; which I did but felt none of the old tingling excitement, the old feeling of being just two in a world of fools that I had experienced, if briefly, earlier that year.

CHAPTER TWENTY-THREE

YES, CEDRIC IS STANDING entwined with Fiona, a sharp east wind cutting into the harbour. She breaks away to tip the porter who in herculean manner is carrying no less than three of these pigskin coffins. And she's only coming for ten days, Cedric thinks. What on earth … ? Oh darling, darling, how pleased I am … Who says? Perhaps she (but I don't recall it). Tip the porter for me, darling. Oh yes, of course. Cedric digs deep into his pockets thinking nothing less than half a crown could repay the man dwarfed as he is by his unnecessary burden. She is plump, he notices too, but not obviously pregnant.

'I'm sure it's going to be a boy,' she says, reminding him horribly of the future as the train puffs through Dalkey.

Oh, God, she's outrageous, he feels, in this shabby carriage which smells of cloth, humanity and stale cigarettes. A huge straw hat frames the frank face with its vast mouth and pearly teeth. Her lipstick is orange. But no, she's not all that vulgar he keeps telling himself as the sea blazes into view once more. It's not her fault she speaks with flat vowels and laughs so loudly. She thinks 'left' and reads the right books. Or used to before she hooked the best scholar of the year. His blood speeds. Oh God! what has he done?

She is to have his room – oh, irony – and he has to sleep in what was called his father's dressing room where a cold iron bed has been put up hurriedly. Maria it is who tenders a limp hand on the steps, dropping a welcome from the side of her mouth. She seems to stress silently her indifference to this wildly painted lady whose makeup resembles some of the less upper-class women who follow the hounds. A tiny smear of pink lipstick is all she ever permits herself, and that only on hunting days. Luckily the bags have been left in the station to be picked up later in Pa's Morris Minor.

Mother is more excited. A real live American seems to bring the possibility of Richard's going to Yale a point closer. She dives immediately into her expectations for Richard's future. And Fiona, with the good manners of the west, is an appreciative listener. Cedric is amazed because he expects Mother to turn on her at any minute. He stands in the hall in his invisible manner, one he has invented for himself whenever he is obliged to be with Mother, giving the right puffs of approval where he deems them relevant.

Theresa! How can he meet Theresa's eye when finally the introductions are made? How explain with his mind, his heart, the blunt reality of the situation? He hungers just then for her beautiful face, her tenderness, the slenderness of her limbs and, oh God, how he wishes to wipe this whole episode out of his life. But he is drowned in it. There's no escape now. He feels himself to be in gaol, all the stars of his life cut off from him. Or in some invisible cube, transparent though glassless, through which he cannot break out.

'Yes, dear', or 'I'll show you up.' Up, up, they go, he carrying her light overnight bag (also pigskin but not so conspicuous) and she tripping (don't all Yanks trip?) up ahead, exclaiming, 'How quaint!' at every dust-laden rung of the staircase. He thinks, I was seduced by my own vanity because she knew a thread of my mind. In Oxford my mind was all throbbing with ideas, here it's dead as lettuce soaked in the vinegar of guilt and the need for love.

He sits on her bed watching her unpack matching garments soft as spiders' webs: a black silk dressing gown with a dragon motif down the back; nighties or a nightie pleated and puffed with underskirt and angora jacket in the same anaemic pink.

'What's wrong with being naked?' he says, puffing the nightie into his fist.

'Alone?' she queries from under her long eyelashes, her vast eyes provocatively twinkling round at him.

'You bitch,' he says, throwing her back and rolling down her knickers.

'I don't think we'd better,' she whirls up round him, straightening her hair briskly like one who greets an unexpected caller.

'Oh, shit,' he says, buttoning up his flies.

'You have learnt to swear. I hope you don't in front of Mommy and Daddy.' The long vowels infuriate, more than the sexual rebuff. He just thinks, so what? and waits for his penis to subside.

What does she think of this ambivalent welcome? The quaint old house with its lavatory cistern that whines and gurgles all night long. All this quaintness belonging to a country seeded in time has its charm for a girl whose every nook and cranny is creamed or powdered so that the flesh is as expressionless as the skin of a penny balloon. Cedric doesn't know what she thinks but observes her exclamations of wonder at each new meeting with family members; Richard luckily is home and makes a welcome bridge with his extrovert extravaganzas.

'What pretty hair she has,' they say later when Fiona leaves the room. 'And how charming she has been,' sighs Cedric to himself.

She charms Theresa as follows: 'Cedric has told me so much about you. But gee, how can you tolerate his priggishness?'

A prig? Cedric, who witnesses the scene from behind his mask, has never thought of himself as a prig. Impatience in the face of ignorance, intolerance, but moral superiority, no! Theresa looks at Cedric's non-expression and a tight little smile or rather grimace as though to say 'what next?' makes Cedric more unsettled.

'Darling,' she links him; his lethargy increases.

'You are obviously such a wonderful person. Mommy and Daddy would never allow me to be spoiled like you've spoiled him.'

Theresa has no intention of answering this barb and she busies herself clearing the dining room table. Fiona picks up a rag and follows her around in an endeavour to appear helpful. 'And his waistline,' she continues. 'How well you've been feeding him since I saw him last. Not that he's fat but he's even more cuddly than ever.'

Cedric leaves the room. He leans on the tall-boy outside the door, hearing Theresa's 'If I were you I'd take him for a walk down the beach while the sun is warm. It's an unsettled-looking sky.' Make hay while the sun shines, Cedric thinks. 'August is a bad month,' Theresa finishes bitterly.

Cedric moves a little down the hall, his chest squeezed like a nut in a nut-cracker. As Fiona steps solidly out of the dining room with 'Theresa says we need a walk,' and a swish of hips audible in silk or satinette, he's ready to agree to anything rather than remain voyeuristic in this neutered state.

The sea has lost its sheen and growls opaquely as each wave crashes on the shingle. The sun only marginally warms them as they drag their feet towards the café. She pulls out her cardigan, which she wears like a cape, and he rubs his hands together – he has bad circulation and death is inching up his fingers. He wonders if Mrs Ribena, the Italian café owner, can be persuaded to give them a pot of tea. He looks longingly at the sand-white ramp running up to the shanty buildings, the tables under their spread of oilcloth, and he imagines the warmth of an earthenware pot round which he could twine his freezing fingers. Fiona is probably wondering when he'll say or do something friendly to her, but he says, 'Bloody Irish climate. Overcoat weather in August as usual. Theresa was right, it's going to lash.'

'Lash?'

'Yes. Lash.'

He suddenly remembers Carmel, warm day, pleated white skirt and a face in its puppyness, but nevertheless not all that unlike Fiona's with the broad mouth, heavy hair and unyielding eyes – Hollywood material all right; and he wishes he were as sterile as a stone.

A distant figure all this time has been intriguing him; on this cold morning they don't expect to see anyone. But the figure, now as they near it, reveals itself as a joyless tramp, thin breasted, a lined face like the shell of a tortoise and female. She has, he notices, beneath strong grey hair a square ugly jaw and a squat nose that has taken punishment in its day. She is creating a little fire, methodical in her building; smaller pieces of driftwood and then a large plank to the windward under which her collection of picnickers' rubbish is bundled and ready to ignite.

He halts Fiona, unwilling to get involved with the tramp's begging and at the same time ashamed at his lack of good will.

'Let's try the café for a cup of tea,' and he turns abruptly.

But Fiona drags. 'Oughtn't we to give her something? Poor old thing?' The fire has caught now and a wisp of smoke races towards them. The driftwood catches quickly and she produces from within her massive clothing a can, and with another dive like a monkey scratching its fur, out comes a bottle from which she drinks, quickly restoring it to its voluminous hiding place.

'No,' he says rudely but is now curious to see what she will do with the can. Will she make tea, for instance? His great investment in his own survival ability is becoming more and more remote. This old hag, this ancient penniless crone, is better off at this minute than he. But no! She again rummages and like a conjuror used to applause produces a new packet from within her garments. A wrap of scraps that she must have begged on her travels, which she now empties into the can which she places slightly to the side of the heat. This done she sits back and takes another swig from her bottle. 'To be always half-drunk is an enviable condition,' he says. 'Shall we go on the razzmatazz tonight?' And for the first time he smiles fully at his future wife.

I remember Fiona was unwilling to drink because of 'her condition' and Cedric had to be content with emptying the decanter after dinner every night when the family had retired to the drawing room.

The old woman has now risen and is hurling herself in their direction, her broken shoes catching in the pebbles and her ankles twisting. She holds out both her hands as though they might throw a coin and it would spin through her fingers. Cedric cannot but dive into his pockets for a sixpence or a few pennies, turning the money over to feel the bevelled edges and calculate the worth. And then in a moment of fury he brings out all his change and deliberately places it in the woman's hands. He turns away terrified of the cringing and 'God-bless-yous' that he knows to expect. He has been overgenerous, fearing Fiona's scalding sneers, and he feels a fool.

CHAPTER TWENTY-FOUR

YOU MUST THINK IT STRANGE that Cedric had so much difficulty in parting with a few lousy shillings but he had always been chilled to the bone by tramps. For a long time as a child he had had a recurring dream of being chased by one and his feet being sucked down and down and he unable to escape. And this fear he had never thrown off.

'Don't encourage them,' had been his mother's dictum all his life, 'or they'll be here every day.' True of course. But it wasn't really the money that cost him a thought although in fact he was always short of cash in those days. It was a deep and personal guilt with which he had to grapple and it wasn't until he was quite old and only too aware of the poverty in the Third World as it is now called that he could speak man to man with someone for whose condition he couldn't help but feel responsible. However, that is only my comment, or my excuse if you like, as I look back on the actions of that callous young man.

CHAPTER TWENTY-FIVE

THEY ARE RETURNING QUICKLY NOW, having foregone the pot of tea. Fiona is encouraged by his recent smile and talks of her hopes for the future, her hopes for the astonishing career with which she has endowed in advance her fiancé. 'You could be almost anything,' she says girlishly after a short and familiar questionnaire about his immediate plans.

'A deep-sea diver, an overhead-crane driver? A doctor, a lawyer, a priest? A scrum-half for Ireland? Or a baseball player for one of your favourite teams?'

'Oh, do be a baseball player and I'll root for you every game.'

'An ace motorist? An Olympic ice-hockey player?'

'Oh Cedric, do be sensible.'

'Why?'

'We have responsibilities.'

'If you must know, I've got a job.'

She is lamentably excited. 'You didn't tell me!'

'No, I was keeping it a secret.'

'Well, are you going to tell me now?'

'Why not? I've got a job as what Jess calls a cub reporter.'

'In Ireland. Oh, love, how exciting!'

'No. In London.'

'But Cedric, the war. You promised.'

'I promised nothing,' he shouts, 'except to marry you.'

And he speeds up his steps so as she has to run to keep up with him.

Yes, he is being exceptionally cruel. And the more he tries not to be the worse it gets. He is sarcastic when he's not being downright rude.

Theresa takes him to task. But he nearly cries when she criticises him and Theresa knows, as she always does, that Cedric is suffering more deeply and in a quite different way from Fiona. Besides, she thinks, to hell with Fiona!

'We used to discuss everything under the sun,' Cedric says morosely. 'And laugh. Yes, I think the laughter is what I miss most. We used to lie in bed giggling half the night.'

'That's the way it goes.'

'Yes. But why so quickly? Why so quickly, Theresa, my love?'

I have drawn a very scanty picture of Fiona. Very unfair, too. She was an intelligent girl but how in the name of God was she supposed to cope with this 'home' Cedric. This alien personality that seemed bent on destroying everything, nipping all her hopes in the bud? This dour Protestant family made no effort to entertain her after the first day or so. Richard only stayed a few days and was off around the country involved in this and that sporting activity. Mother retreated into her cocoon (her newspapers, her wireless), seldom rising before twelve and spending most of the afternoon cooped up in the drawing room with the curtains half-drawn. Maria, when not out riding, spent most of her day on the step reading. Or else she too would disappear, to paint her views, I afterwards discovered. Theresa spoke kindly to her whenever they met, but it was usually a moment in the hall, in the corridor upstairs or in the kitchen when Cedric deliberately brought her down there. Cedric too began to make excuses, correspondence to be caught up with, research into this and that which meant going to town to sit in the National Library, so the poor girl was left to her own devices. I think she spent much time on the beach. Killiney beach does that kind of thing to you. You can walk for miles along the stones and on cold days see nary a soul. The old yellow cliffs exclude the sun soon after four o'clock and it is a damp and dismal place thereafter. Occasionally a hardy family might venture down and the youngsters strip shivering and scream into the sea. But the east wind never ceased that August.

When it came to the time for them to leave, Cedric was shut into himself like a tortoise into its shell.

> It is not, as some people appear to think, sufficient for us to indicate our attitude, or to express the desire of our people. It is necessary at every step to protect our own interests in that regard, to avoid giving to any of the belligerents any due cause, any proper cause of complaint. Of course, when you have powerful states in a war of this sort, each trying to utilise whatever advantage it can for itself, the neutral State, if it is a small State, is always open to considerable pressure. I am stating what every one of you knows to be a fact. Therefore, when I was speaking of our policy of neutrality on a former occasion, I said it was a policy which could only be pursued if we had a determined people, a people determined to stand by their own right, conscious of the fact that they did not wish to injure anybody, or to throw their weight, from the belligerent point of view, on the one side or the other.

Listening to de Valera's speech Cedric felt a loosening of the arteries as though his blood had begun to flow freely after being dammed up for months. And when war was declared the following day he began throwing stuff into his suitcase, jettisoning half of it afterwards when the lid wouldn't shut. Fiona packed her pretty clothes too, happily enough. Perhaps she hoped that with the possibility of their being alone things would improve between them. Also the marriage. It was arranged for the fifteenth of September and her parents would arrive the week before. There would be hotel accommodation to arrange. So they departed on a packed mail boat – there was much shuffling across the Irish Sea in those early war years, in fact all through the war, when smuggling was one of the happiest outcomes of those horrendous years.

However, this is not, as I have said before, exactly the story of Cedric; I have written elsewhere about my war experiences in any case. I came home three times. Therefore this bleak and exciting period has nothing to do with the present narrative.

CHAPTER TWENTY-SIX

IT IS 1946 WHEN WE FINALLY pick up the threads.
Cedric is sitting with Theresa on a garden seat. The
weeds have not been tended and long scutch grasses tickle
their knees, shine wet in the sun. Cedric says, 'Yes. I got the
telegram when under one of Rommel's most vicious attacks.
Not that I was scathed! Some of us journalists had a cushy
war all the same.'

'Nothing very cushy about the desert campaign,' Theresa
says.

Theresa looks well although her expression is a little
drawn. She has worried all through the war and she confides
to Cedric that if he had been killed there would have been
little choice for her but to leave the Stewart family.

'Going into Italy was fun,' he says. 'Seeing Rome like that.
Everything on the black market if you could afford it, half
the country starving. Black, Theresa, black, but it suited
my horrible temperament. I think, Theresa, if I'd been born
poor I'd have made a first-class criminal.' He kisses her ear to
bring that smile that he often thought of as a child to be like
the solution to a difficult mathematical problem. For hours
you puzzle and then suddenly you hit on the answer. Yes,
her smile is a solution, he thinks. 'Yes. Getting the two
telegrams one on top of the other was probably the worst
thing that happened to me during the whole war. I kept
seeing Father and his poor emotional face and his inability to

speak. I saw him trailing the funerals stiffly, tidily, in his Crombie or old herring-bone tweed. His eyes dry except when the east wind got at them.'

'He cried openly at Maria's funeral. I never saw a man so distressed. He was such a held-in man normally. Is still. Just that once, it seems, he let go.'

'I never told you how I found him crying on the stairs. It had such a horrible effect on me that I had to keep it to myself. I never told even you.'

'Sure, I hardly saw you at all that summer. You were so unsure about everything. You had to withdraw into your shell to try to sort things out.'

Cedric is almost afraid to talk of Jess's death. He is afraid of the renewed agony that will strike him now as he walks past her empty room: how he'll miss her fussy whine, her giggle when finally he'd dragged her out of self-pity into a vehement and acid humour which she could perfect when she felt up to it. He tentatively asks did her religion help her at all.

'I don't know. She didn't want to die. I know that. She threw out Father Conlon and he had to bumble down the stairs like a man caught with his flies open. Easiest thing for those damned buggers bringing the last rites and they in the pink. And your father. I think they nearly drove him over the edge. He used to fume and fret and pace the room when they were around. They were like a swarm of bees. I hope when I go, I go before they get at me.'

Cedric is relieved. He doesn't quite know why. His sister's fighting the priests seems in a way a good sign. She fought for herself to the end, he feels. Threw them out when they were no more use.

'I'm glad,' he says simply. 'The "turned" Catholic is a hard nut.'

Yes. There is much to say. So much that he looks forward to this long uncluttered summer. He plans to stay out of his parents' way as much as possible. He is quite glad to tell Theresa his marriage is washed up. 'The war and the long parting has done for us. Is it as well? She prefers her home in Boston to my lovely Chelsea flat. And it is lovely. I wasn't idle. I picked up some odds and ends. The old British tradition of stealing art treasures. Further, the *Sunday News* has taken me on as an art critic. So if I praise the good artists, dot dot dot! Do you think I'm immoral?'

'I make no judgements.'

'I should think not!' He kisses again her ear. 'Oh, Theresa, my love, I wish I had married you.'

'What will you do about your boys?'

'One of them's at some sort of all-American pre-High and the other at some pre-Low or something. In Boston. Happy, I gather. But you didn't answer my question.'

'What?'

'Had married you.'

'Had things been different and I younger.'

'James Joyce married a maid.'

'He didn't *marry* her.'

'Don't be obtuse. And he did in the end.'

'Richard's expected for supper.'

'Don't change the subject. It's not too late.'

'Some things are.'

'No. Theresa, no. My love. You know who I thought about in the desert while I was listening to "Lili Marlene"?'

Theresa begins to get up sideways as though to relinquish emotion without hurt to either. 'I must go.'

'No, no. For God's sake, don't leave me.'

'Shh. Your mother can hear us from the drawing room.'

'I don't give a f...fig if she does; my love, will you ... ?'

She is fully risen now and stands above him; she says desolately, 'Let me go now,' and walks away, her feet dragging back from him for he has snatched her hand. But he doesn't look up as her fingers slide through his and he hears the swish, swish receding down the lawn, the three steps up and the hall door opening and closing.

He leans down and stirs the weeds with his feet, his elbows clamped on his knees. He spreads a dandelion, plucking at the last moment the yellow flower and remembers a day of buttercups and holding one under Jess's chin, laughing, 'You like butter. Who likes butter? See, you do.'

Beside the drawing room is a room seldom used. It is a non-room, like an annexe to the hall, in which the telephone apparatus hangs and in which a glass-fronted case contains some books with gilt-edged spines: the works of Dickens, Thackeray, Sir Walter Scott. Some of the collections are out of order, missing a volume here and there; they are in his room. He is standing at the telephone; he calls in the number to the girl at the switchboard in Ballybrack. A well-schooled voice repeats it and sparking sounds are emitted from the earpiece till a thin 'hullo' almost pierces his eardrum.

'Can I speak to Miss McDonnell? I believe she works there. Oh ... Carmel? It's you ... Cedric Stewart here ... Yes ... Long time ... Oh ... all right, I suppose.' He laughs. 'I got no medals! Do you feel like a movie tonight ... ? Where ... ? In Westland Row opposite the station there's a hotel. Meet you in the lobby ... Yes? Around half past six? OK. I will. Promise.' He replaces the receiver and stares belligerently at the telephone. His mother pokes her head in.

'Who are you phoning, Cedric dear?'

'A friend, Mother.'

'Oh.' She lingers. He, too.

'Yes. An old college friend who's in Dublin for a break.'

'You didn't tell me.'

'He's only passing through.'

'Oh, what a pity. It would have been nice for you to have him out for dinner.'

Cedric murmurs incoherently. So all my friends are male. He likes to think that one day in Ireland a married man will be able to meet a woman for a cup of tea without being flayed by subterfuge and guilt.

The avenue glistens as he walks down, his one suit feeling rather tight. It is of good pre-war tweed, brown with a yellow fleck. His tie is green tweed and his hat, an old deer-stalker stolen off Father's peg, makes, he feels, his appearance pleasantly flamboyant. He lacks only a silver-topped cane.

The train is late: he taps the platform impatiently with his wide brown walking shoe, noticing as he does so that it could have done with a rub. The platform also glistens, little puddles having formed between the flags after a recent shower. But the east wind, thank God, has dropped and he feels warm, perhaps too warm, this July afternoon. But the weather has been squally lately, as the station-master has just remarked in passing. Cedric notices that he is getting on in years now. He was never his favourite man, tending to snide remarks when Cedric was a boy. Cedric had feared his tongue and was wont to run on to the train as quickly as possible in order to avoid what he interpreted as a veiled sneer which encompassed the station-master's opinion about the Stewart family in general. Snobs, in other words.

'Well, we were,' Cedric thinks, 'and there's no way that I can change his opinion of us. I can't very well say, "Listen, old boy, we're all cut in the same cloth when you boil it down. It's just that Protestants are terrified of Catholics and adopt this reserved attitude for self-protection."'

Further, the station-master was an unprepossessing individual. A ludicrously enlarged lower lip made him look as though he had been stung by a wasp and his pipe, always empty, made an unattractive gurgling sound as it hung from his mouth, clamped firmly between black and battered teeth.

'Thank heaven,' Cedric thinks, 'he is too busy at the moment to speak to me.' He is readying a heap of parcels for the five-thirty and is about to shunt his trolley back to the shed for more.

Sitting in the train later, Cedric counts the different colours of the houses in Sorrento Terrace, reckoning that they are pleasant in that mid-Victorian manner: decayed, old-seaside, standing up to wind and weather. Old people in wraps, rugs to their chins, breathe in the sea air and will do so, he hopes, till replaced by another generation. And he wonders is he just becoming a traditionalist, a conservative capitalist, hell-bent on making money, wheeler-dealing under the guise of being an expert – his erudite and carefully annotated book, just now ready for a publisher, simply a cover-up for a rather dull life ahead. But no, he shouts silently at a passing gull, when summer ends he'll be off to find out, to talk and dig while always keeping that clever eye of his wide open.

Westland Row, its blunt end dirty as ever, greets him before his thoughts have half-run through their tunnel and he alights a little circumspectly, avoiding a puddle of vomit that some unfortunate mail-boater deposited earlier on the platform. He is too early for Carmel and he strolls into the evening street possessed of a desire for alcohol which he has lately noticed increasing in his metabolism. The nearest pub is actually the hotel and he enters hoping that the girl won't be early and he'll have time to knock back a few smart ones before they meet.

The bar, dark, is to the left of the hall and he takes up a position in which he'll see her before she sees him.

When she does arrive he's shocked. Not because she's old and ugly – only thirty, after all – but because her expression has changed. Her curiosity, her most endearing quality, has been superseded by obviously false self-confidence. As if with her first glance she is saying: 'I know what all men are after.' But, yes, physically also she has changed. She has become flowing, almost matronly, heavy below and above her waist. Her face, apart from its expression, is as it was, model to perfection. But there's something else which suddenly hits him: she is more Dublin-ish than he remembers. He greets her quickly, overenthusiastically, jumping from his stool, holding out his hand with which he leads her to the bar and the seat beside his; 'What'll you have?'

She demurs, says she doesn't drink.

'An orange soda, a ginger beer, a Pimms Number One?'

'I never heard of that.'

'Scotch and water and a Pimms Number One,' he tells the barman, an elderly gent who looks as though he's always been in the wrong profession.

'Are all Irish youth sex mad?' he asks her when the barman is out of earshot.

'I beg your pardon?'

'No. It's just that you look very nervous.' She doesn't actually, but he wants to crack her confident veneer quickly so that the evening may be bearable.

He hopes, too, that the Pimms will give her an internal glow, make her perhaps believe that those old tennis-playing summers once existed. Make her giggle and twirl around, make those large lips part into an easy grin.

He wants to scream.

'What would you like to do?'

'Aren't we going to the pictures?' And then, 'I'm hungry.'

'Let's have a bite, so,' he says. 'There's a café not far where we can plan our evening.' The wide lips do part at last.

'The war has been terrible,' she says.

'How so?'

'I'd have liked to go to England to join the ATS but Daddy wouldn't let me.'

'Poor you.'

'I suppose you were doing something intelligent,' she says, as though she's afraid to use the word dangerous.

'It was neither intelligent nor dangerous. I trailed after Montgomery miles away from the enemy lines. Sending despatches back to London, making indecipherable notes, living in incredible discomfort – that's about the height of it.'

'Poor thing.'

The conversation is drooping, he thinks, as he steers her out and into the café.

Here the waitress, a really bad-tempered girl, brings two plates of Welsh rabbit and a pot of tea.

'Not exactly the Ritz. We should have gone somewhere – well, a bit more exciting.'

'Oh, I don't mind.' The alcohol has relaxed her partially. 'I come here most Friday evenings before taking the train home.'

'Do you go home every weekend?'

'Not every weekend.' There is a sudden gust of laughter which is hatefully out of place in these sordid surroundings.

'Would you like some toast? I'm sure we could have toast,' he says, trying to stop her laughing. He feels as though a sink has overflowed and he's trying to catch the water in a bucket. But she continues to laugh, 'Good heavens no, you won't get toast here.'

'Toast!' he almost screams, and the waitress looks up, a loop of lank hair falling back to her neck. 'We don't do toast,' she says, not moving any nearer.

Carmel's laughter stops as though it never was.

'I told you so.'

She pours herself a third cup of tea and points the spout at Cedric, her eyebrows raised.

'No thanks,' he says to the unspoken offer. 'Let's go.'

'Can I just finish this cup?'

Cedric doesn't answer. He tries not to scowl, to look patient, expectant, friendly. He tries to think 'Poor Carmel' instead of 'Fuck her!'

'What picture would you like to see?' she says now, thoroughly pleased at her minor victory.

'I thought that perhaps we might, er, go to your place for a quiet evening. To fill in the blanks.'

'What blanks?'

'In our mutually invisible past. I tell mine and you tell yours.'

'My girl friend will be in and I think you'd find her rather stupid.'

'Do you find her stupid?'

'Of course not. But it's different for me.'

'Tell me?'

'I can't.' Her pseudo-confidence is all gone now; all pretence subsided into a muddle of apprehension. 'Why did you ask me out tonight? You were often home during the war and you never bothered.' He's mildly surprised. She must have kept up her interest in him. So now she uncurls a thread of his cruelty, does she?

'I don't know,' he says. 'I would like another drink. This place is destructive.'

'I don't drink, I told you. But I'll come with you, if you like.'

'Do you dislike me?' he asks.

'Why should I?' Carmel is visibly shaken by this volte-face.

'I don't know. I treated you pretty shabbily long ago.'

'We were kids then.'

He is moved to put his hand over hers; she is a child again faced with his furtive pubertal sexuality.

'Sorry,' he says, very quietly. They leave the café.

In the pub they have to go into the snug: no women allowed in the bar. The snug is like a confessional, hard wooden seats back to the window, a tiny hatch through which one has to get the barman's attention. 'A large Scotch and,' he turns, 'another Pimms?'

'No thank you. It tasted funny. Was there alcohol in it?'

'Perhaps.'

'Well, no … oh, anything,' in a small voice.

'Lemonade,' he says briefly. 'And so you ditched your boyfriend.'

'Boyfriend?'

'What was his name?'

'Oh, George,' Carmel laughs, but this time more quietly, 'I haven't thought about him for years. He works in Dublin somewhere I believe … but … '

'Strange how a handsome woman like yourself … '

'Should be still a spinster? Only part-time boyfriends. I had to put one off tonight after you phoned.'

Cedric sees Theresa sitting at home, fingers interlaced, and his stomach knots. 'Have you ever done anything unforgivable?'

'Told lies to Mummy?'

'No. Not telling lies to Mummy. Betrayed someone so badly in order to flagellate yourself?'

'I don't understand you.'

'Hard to. I wondered. Perhaps everyone does it.'

After his third drink he says, 'Sorry. Forgive me. Why don't you drink. Or anything? You're too bloody nice. Too reasonable. People should never be reasonable. People … Carmel, will you sleep with me? I know this is gauche and men are supposed to build up to this sort of thing with flowers and subtlety but I can't be bothered.' He shouts, 'Another Scotch.'

'Why don't you say please?'

'Because I'm unreasonable.'

'No need to shout at the barman. He's not responsible for your greed.'

'Greed? What an odd word.'

'You think I'm a fool.'

'On the contrary. I have the greatest respect for your mind. But you haven't answered.'

'Answer is no. At least I think it is. Or at least not tonight.'

Cedric feels a spiral of anger running up his chest. 'There won't be another night. I'm leaving in a few days. So.'

★

Looking back on it, as far as I can remember the sordid little episode, I'm sure that Carmel was about to change her mind. But Cedric blew it, as they say now. His supreme arrogance always drove him to absurdities like these.

Carmel gets up and runs out and Cedric shouts after her, 'Thank you for listening to me,' turns back to the table and downs his drink, making dramatic fisticuffs in the direction of the girl, himself, the world.

The door isn't locked. It never is or was, he knows. He tiptoes in and sees the pale, still head on the pillow by the light of a candle he carries. The thin lines round her eyes are like pencil etchings – he remembers a picture of Keats on his deathbed by his friend Leigh Hunt and thinks that she has a neat head like an adolescent boy's. The slight manifestations of age that are apparent during the day sometimes are invisible as she lies here.

Very gently he lowers himself onto the bed, having stripped off his trousers, shoes and jacket. She opens her eyes.

'I never knew,' he says.

'How could you?'

'Lots of people do. Ordinary people. That's not true. I'm probably more ordinary than most. That's the trouble, the misfits are so ordinary the masses hate them.'

'Easy to say.' Cedric kisses down her arm.

'That arm,' he places his hand under her breast. 'That heart.' He strokes her hair. 'That small intelligent head. Theresa. They all belong to *you*, Theresa. No one else. Not me. Not anyone. Just you. And most people never let it go at that.' He lies back, hands under head. 'Am I making sense? The awful germ of possession. Do you know what I did this evening?' The shock of realisation makes him roll over on to

one elbow. 'I went into town and met Carmel and proposi-
tioned her. I'm telling you this not to hurt you but to
reassure you. I hated her all evening. Her fat, silly little body
and her sort of virgin–cum–sophisticated mind. I wanted to
get her drunk – she wouldn't touch it. I wanted to kill her
I think. Well, not really. Well, yes. I think I'd have liked
to kill her because I felt nothing and if I'd killed her at least
I'd have felt hatred. Because when I said I hated her, of
course I didn't. How could anyone hate or love Carmel
McDonnell?

'Do you remember, Theresa, when I used to try and hatch
chrysalises? I kept them in those big matchboxes, collected
caterpillars. And once a deformed butterfly hatched out; I'll
never forget my chagrin. I tried again and again but I never
got a fully fledged butterfly. Before the caterpillars turned I
used to line the box with cabbage leaf. They ate voraciously,
I remember.'

'So you will never hatch your butterfly?'

'No. What I'm trying to tell you is that left to its own
devices the butterfly will hatch itself. Gloriously, with all the
colours of the rainbow. But if I interfere everything is
spoiled. You were there before me, all your different parts,
the twists and turns of your mind.'

It is Theresa's turn to rise on an elbow and stroke the wet
hair that has a mixture of grease and rain in it. It smells of
root vegetables. 'Shsh,' she says.

Looking up straight at her, for they are face to face now,
he says, 'There's no shushing now. I'm going. Going to
Burma. To work. To work till I fall down dead in my tracks.
Like the old man. The old man knows. It's only work that
counts. Work, work, work. And I'm the laziest man I know.
What's it all to do with us, my love?'

The night wears on. They talk till the first birds and Cedric
says, 'Oh God, now I've kept you awake all night and you
have to toil and moil for our lousy family all day. Stay in bed,

my love, and I'll cook and clean; I'll tell Mother you're not well.'

'I think,' Theresa says, 'that I am well. Perhaps more full of well-being than I've been for a long time. But we'll sleep now for a couple of hours and then you can well help me with the worst of the chores.'

Yet it seems only a minute later that they are standing in the kitchen leaning against the Aga with tea cups ringed with their fingers, the smudge on Theresa's forehead from aggravating the cooker like the mark of Ash Wednesday. Pa, whom Cedric has scarcely spoken to since his arrival, can be heard poking about upstairs. He has had his breakfast, served as usual on a tray in the sitting room, and the dog, always restless at his departure, can be heard pattering up and down the hall, whining in between small exasperated yaps.

'Ah, little doggie,' the old man says.

'How he loves that tattered little rat,' Cedric says. 'The only living thing to whom he can openly show affection.

'And he never hunted since Maria died, you say? I think that's terrible. At least he was free flying round on that awful old horse. Free of his office imprisonment, his familial worries.'

'He gave the horse to Jim. That was an end to it.'

Cedric feels the need to drift away. He can't stay all day in the kitchen but he feels if he leaves her side she'll disappear as if by magic; he'll lose her as though she were merely a manifestation of something he thought he never had: a soul.

'The seagulls are in. There'll be a storm,' Theresa says.

It is late afternoon. Theresa is fresh from a short sleep: a muslin blouse, coffee-coloured, offsets her light brown skin; she is new hay to his nostrils as he catches her once more in the kitchen, hand on waist.

Mother calls, 'Cedric!'

'Say I'm not here,' he whispers.

'He's not down here, Mrs Stewart.'

'How very annoying!'

Cedric holds his breath dramatically. As her steps recede he exhales. 'I wish to hell Richard were here to take the weight off my back.'

'He'll never fill the gap you leave unfilled with the two old people.'

'Oh I know, I know. Do you know what they said of Chekhov? He never opened his soul to anyone. He was a cold man, I believe; his wife was sexually unsatisfied so finally she took a lover. And that was a fiasco, too. She was sexually accident prone because apparently she was extraordinarily attractive. Perhaps he was impotent. Do you think I'll end up an impotent old man chasing young girls in corridors? Oh, God, I feel like going out and getting drunk. Not with Carmel. On my own. There's nothing else to do.'

'Stay and talk to me. You wash the dishes.'

'Oh Theresa, you're so wise. Bring me down with a bump. I can't live with women and I can't live without them.'

'You're not the first.'

'It's all right for Richard. He and Sheila ... '

'He's not as contented as you think. Anyway, they're not married yet.'

'They will be. I should come over, I suppose. But I'll be far away. Yes, far away from you, my love. And them.' He raises his eyes to indicate upstairs. 'Flirting with some horrible magistrate's wife. Or magistrate's horrible wife. Or flattering her. God, I'm horrible.'

'Stop.'

'I've never loved anyone, have I, Theresa? Mother, Jess, Pa, my wife, Maria ... '

'Me. You love me.'

He stops washing and stares round at her. 'No!' He wipes his face with his wrist.

'Yes. You do love me!'

He turns back to the plates. 'What a funny conversation. Come for a walk down the beach. I think the rain is off for a while.'

'The unit I was attached to had two artists, a composer and at least four published writers.' He picks up a stone and throws it into the waves. 'They're all dead.'

'You had someone to talk to.'

'Yes. About food and women. Hypothetical food and hypothetical women. One of the writers, Williams, used to conjure up the most succulent dishes – down to the last detail.' He hurls another stone into the water. 'We had to shut him up. At least until the Germans did.'

'You could have as easily been killed as the others.'

'All luck, Theresa, all luck.'

'Your father used to watch the post every day. Sometimes went down to the gate. He was worse after Maria died. Sometimes used to accuse the postman of losing non-existent letters.'

'So strange. I think you make these things up. To please me.' He kisses her cheek, lacing his fingers round her waist. 'To keep on my right side.'

She smiles. 'Maybe.'

'Funny you've never met my children. A whole era of me that you know nothing about. Well, a very short era, admittedly. An era, nevertheless. And there's going to be another one now. Another new me era. But I'll know what you're doing, Theresa.'

'You won't have to stretch your imagination.'

'Do you know what worries me? When I'm away?'

'That I'll be dead?'

'Not dead. I wouldn't mind if you were dead. But married. That some swine would suddenly appear and realise what he's been missing all his life. Some middle-aged balding bastard with a bank account.'

'Some hope. If it hasn't happened by now at my age.'

'If a young man of twenty-nine wants to get into bed with a young woman of forty-two, what wouldn't an old widower give for the privilege?'

'And how will you live? How about your job on the Sunday?'

'I'll work it out. I'll deal. My first book is ready for the publisher. I have to collate some facts. How pedantic that all sounds. I'm a crook with an eye for the main chance. I must get there before the Americans get there and fill their collections in Boston and New York. I've no intention of giving up my lovely Chelsea flat. Do you know when I lie in bed listening to the traffic I occasionally fancy I can hear the sea. And vice versa. When I lie in bed at home I sometimes fancy the sea sounds like the noise of King's Road.'

'Do your parents know you're going so soon?'

They have reached the white rock and Cedric looks at Theresa long and mournfully. 'The tide is turning. We'll be caught.'

'There's always a way round.' A train edges slowly along the line above their heads. 'One day the cliff will fall and the whole line will come tumbling down,' she says.

Those were three days and three nights. Did we make love within the meaning of the word? And yet it wasn't just a lacuna: it was a continuation, a dip or a rise in the graph of our relationship. But I haven't answered my question and I'm afraid the more prurient readers will have to remain unsatisfied. I've no intention of writing in the sexual details. All I know is that when cynics tell me there is no such thing as perfect love I'm wont to smile secretly. The last evening and morning ended on a dying fall; some of it has been recounted to me by Theresa herself.

Richard comes into the hall blowing rude health all round him. He is a much more attractive young man than the gawkish adolescent whom Cedric likened to a eunuch. He has that squashed Stewart face – high cheekbones, heavy eyelids – but now in his twenty-sixth year he exudes a defiant charm, a warm-heartedness, as always extrovert, that even Cedric finds hard to resist.

'Cedric, old chap. Welcome home. And alas, I believe, goodbye. I'm so sorry that we couldn't have had more time together.'

'So am I,' and he means it; a moment of puzzlement: 'Your fiancée? Not with you?'

'I'm reconciled.'

'To what? To being a bachelor?'

'No. To being married. And no. She's with her parents in Sligo. A bank manager's daughter has to pay lip-service occasionally. Just as I … '

'*You* don't mean it. You are as attached to this place as I am.' Cedric wonders is he; or is he, himself? Or only to one person or the personification of? He is suddenly aware of collapse, he feels heavy: a tree that's about to be felled.

He envies Richard's energy which is all about him.

'I'll be earning good money in London,' Richard says.

'Does Mother know?'

'Not yet.'

'How are you going to tell her?'

'I'll distil the information with exuberant explanations of salary, commitment, etcetera.'

'You're young to be a consultant.'

'A question of degree, dear fellow. You're young when you feel young.'

'I feel old in this house.'

'You were never a child.'

So in his innocence he has hit the nail on the head. Never cuddled by his parents! All that Freudian piffle! But perhaps it's what Richard likes.

'No. You were a little old man poking into books, listing the names of snails and shell-fish.'

'I spent most of my childhood in the kitchen.' But no, this is too near; a crumpled leaf which is already tucked into the book of his continued existence. 'That is to say, keeping out of draughts.'

Richard lifts his heavy eyelids a fraction. 'I was too sporting for you. No company, I'm afraid.'

'Perhaps we both miss James.'

'Ah, James.' They are stagnant now in the hall. 'I'll go back in to Mother. Break the news.'

Cedric wanders out into the garden. Everything pleases him. The marrows saffron, glinting their swollen bodies in the sunshine. Raspberries, red thimbles. Weeds popping up here and there. Old Barton only manages one day a week now. He strokes some weeds from the canes, gently, as though stroking long hair from a woman's brow. The young apple trees, so lovingly spliced by his father long ago, are beginning to flower. It will be a good crop this autumn, he thinks.

He hesitates by the back wall where the clematis is being choked by robin-run-in-the-hedge. He pulls to uproot a clump of the sticky weed and some petals fall on his shoulder. He shakes them into his hand and wonders should he make a posy for his mother on this his last evening in the house for many moons. The flowers don't break off easily and he decides that they should be left as they are to live through their own cycle without his interference.

He knows he should be in the kitchen helping Theresa. It's to be a special dinner tonight. He hears his father coming up the kitchen garden.

'Richard's home,' he calls.

His father looks up at his eldest son. In the blinding western light his father's face is the colour of fig. He needs to be more out of doors, Cedric thinks. Never a man to coop himself up. He lets the whole distressful past slide down on him like slag on a slag heap. But like the clematis that won't leave its stalk Cedric is unable to pluck his father from his self-inflicted imprisonment.

One day the mourning must end, Cedric thinks. But when? But when? And the thought of the possible death of one of his own sons, although he may not see them for years, empties his belly like a bucket of milk being emptied into a hollow milk-churn. So how expect his father to forget his double loss?

'How well the clematis blooms this year, Father,' he adds.

'The weeds have nearly choked it,' the old man says.

His father's lack of enthusiasm makes Cedric feel insipid when he should feel pugnacious. He should pick up his father and shake him like shaking earth out of a parsnip. But he just stands deflated until the old man continues his journey towards the house.

His pleasure is all gone now, even the physical joy in eating peas from the living pod. He takes one more look at the garden, wondering will there be anything here at all when he's home again. Not that he plans a very long stay away but he feels that the world will turn more quickly when he passes his thirtieth birthday.

He sees, suddenly, Maria, as she might be were she still alive. He seldom saw her on a horse but he sees her now, her straight back, her bowler hat tilted a little over that dowdy face. He sees her cantering along a field, clods of earth raining behind the horse's hooves. He sees the long flowing mane, his sister's right hand with kid glove holding rein and crop, moving with the movement of the horse. She pulls up at a gate, sits back in the saddle and takes off her hat. Her fair hair which has been squashed down by the bowler clings to her head like a bathing cap. She half smiles from the enjoyment of the gallop. For a moment she looks like James.

She would be thirty-one now and prematurely elderly. Or would she have married? Someone met on the hunting field? No. She was the greatest snob of them all, or perhaps more frightened of class than any of them. No buccaneer of a farmer's son would have matched up to her idea of a suitable husband. She would have wanted to move up a shade, even. Away from the professional class into the landed dimension. A private income rather than a few bob handed out from Father whenever he could spare it. And Father was excessively generous with her, he remembers. Frequently Mother had ranted and raved about the money spent on Maria's horses but Pa always turned the other cheek and continued to dole out money in large quantities. He enjoyed the hunt himself, so why blame him? He is more to blame now for denying himself his pleasures in this mournful manner.

Later, I discovered that Father blamed himself for Maria's death. He said that if he had noticed her earlier lying on the ground he could have saved her. This is ridiculous, of course, because her skull was fractured and death was instantaneous.

But Maria has galloped out of sight forever and they will never meet again for those embarrassing silences. There had never been any banter between them as between him and Jess. Speech to Maria was high-toned, moral. The tight layer of disapproval with which she looked on all forms of human weakness was her only defence against her deeply frustrated artistic soul being bared to others. Yet Cedric suddenly mourns his sister Maria as he has never mourned the loss of

Jess. Someone he never knew, nor ever tried to know. Someone over whom he had felt a shocking intellectual superiority. Had she been allowed to talk, or had he forced her to, their relationship might have been forged into being.

The evening is heavy now, the garden dark, the sun having dropped over the hill. Only the back windows of McDonnell's house, he thinks cynically, will be lit by its sinking rays. It is shivery here, yet he feels the need to stay out of the house until the gong sounds for dinner. But he's too cold. He came out in his open-necked short-sleeved Aertex shirt and it clings damply to him like chain mail.

He wanders back in through the kitchen door but Theresa isn't there. A flash of guilt. He had promised to lay the table at least.

In the dining room the table, he's glad to see, is still bare and he sets about with the silver: soup spoon on the outside, then the two bone-handled knives on the right. On the left a small and a large silver fork – the larger ones EPNS, not Georgian – and the pudding spoon and fork on the top like a crown. The round cork mats, over which he places the shivering lace. Then the tumblers, wine glasses and finally the candelabra. He looks pleasurably at his handiwork.

He remembers how after Christmas dinner the children used to play charades: they had been allowed wine and were full of shrieks and laughter at their own inventiveness. Once he chose CHRYSALIS and when directing the last syllable he insisted on having a corpse in the middle of the stage which suddenly wakes up. And they mime excitement to infer that Christ *is* instead of *isn't*. The great-uncles and aunts – there were always plenty of those – said it wasn't fair and Mother said it was in bad taste. But he remembered that Pa had smiled indulgently. He kept good-tempered all through those many Christmases, allowing the children as much rope as they wanted that one day a year.

'You remembered,' Theresa is bringing in the soup tureen.

'I heard you rattling about so I didn't bother coming up to check.'

On this last night they stand like strangers. They are afraid. They have shut their minds against the imminent parting. It is just another one. They will write. They always have written. Long jokey, newsy scrawls.

'I went out into the garden. I didn't notice the time passing.'

'You thought.'

'Yes. A lot. About Maria, mostly.'

'Yes.'

'Would her life have followed its bleak course, had she lived? An old spinster at thirty-one?'

Theresa doesn't answer; she is forty-two, unmarried herself.

She turns her back to him, pretends business at the side-table.

'You are not … ' he says, dismayed at his carelessness. 'You aren't married because there's no one good enough for you. Oh, God, love. Don't let's say anything more.'

If she smiles, he thinks, I'll go in peace. She does.

'Marriage would have been important to Maria, is what I meant.'

'I know,' she smiles again. 'Bang the gong, will you?'

How he used to love this task when he was a child.

CHAPTER TWENTY-SEVEN

'YES, I HAVE DECIDED.' Richard is crumbling his bread roll, his pudding plate empty in front of him. 'I'll take more raspberries,' he adds, getting up and going to the sideboard.

'I thought you were going to stay on in the children's hospital in Dublin,' Mother says, her voice tormented.

'It won't be for some time, Mother. We're getting married first.'

Cedric offers his father more wine which he refuses. He fills his own glass.

Richard inclines towards his brother, having returned to his seat.

'When is your boat, old man?'

'I must catch the seven o'clock train. The boat leaves at eight-thirty.'

'How very inconvenient,' Mother says. 'Could you not go on the night boat?'

'I'll get myself up, Mother.' Cedric laughs lightly.

'You are being very selfish.'

'I'll bid my adieus tonight. There's no need for you to think you have to rise.'

'Of course Mother can't be dragged out of bed at that hour.'

'Nobody's dragging anybody out of bed. Especially you, Father, since you rise at seven-thirty yourself every morning.'

'I do think you should please Mother on this occasion. What possible difference can it make to you if you go in the evening?' Richard adds.

Cedric looks for Theresa but she has her back to him. When there is a mumble of 'coffee', he jumps up. 'I'll get it,' he says and goes from the room.

Father looks mournfully after him. 'It grieves me that there should be bickering on the night before my eldest son's departure. He was prevented from going east all through the war. Now that it is possible he is naturally impatient to leave. No doubt there are things he must attend to in London and it is most thoughtless of you both to upset him like this. I know in the past I tried to discourage him in his projects and I was wrong.' He pauses to take his empty plate and glass to the sideboard. Mother and Richard look at him in astonishment. Turning towards his wife he says, 'I think, Edith, that we will have to get someone to help Theresa in the kitchen. Will you see to that?' He pauses to wipe his mouth. 'I don't wish to hear any more arguing tonight. I shall pray for Cedric on Sunday. That is all.' He turns towards the door. 'I shall be in my study for the next hour if you need me. You may bring my coffee in to me, Richard.'

As the door closes behind him, Richard and his mother unstiffen slowly. 'Father is being very strange.' Richard exhales cigarette smoke.

'He is not well.'

'Well, Mother? You mean there is something … '

'Perhaps you would look him over before you go?'

'He is as active as ever … I can't imagine … '

'Never mind, dear. We will have our little chat in peace.'

Theresa, who all this time has been concerned with making herself invisible in the periphery of the candlelight, emerges from the shadows and crosses the room like a small but triumphant ghost. Mother and son stare after her as she, too, escapes through the door and goes down to the kitchen where she recounts the gist of the foregoing to Cedric.

Profoundly moved by his father's defence of his principles he looks long and sadly into Theresa's eyes as the coffee bubbles in the percolator. At length, he says, 'In the gloom and the shadows. Poor Father.'

'It cost him a lot to say it,' she says.

Cedric picks up the coffee pot. At the door he turns, one foot hooked round it. 'I'll go to bed early tonight,' he says, not as yet knowing whether they'll sleep together or not.

Birds often appear to wake earlier when you're going to leave a place. The following morning the chorus is deafening. When Cedric wakes he is startled by the music; it is as though hundreds of small bells are being shaken in the trees outside, a triumphal sheet of sound. Theresa's side of the bed is still warm and turning he runs the palm of his hand along the slight hollow left by her body. His clothes, as usual pegged over the floor, give the room a heavenly expression of comfort. He can't – how can he? – leave today. He stretches his legs so that his feet press against the iron bedstead, curling his toes around the bars. His stretched body feels clean and new. He turns on his back and lifts his hands to his chest, twirling a small tuft of hair that grows over his left breast with the index finger of his right hand. 'Oh, God!' he says and throws the bedclothes back.

'Your breakfast is ready, sir,'

'My son?'

'He didn't forget anything, this time.'

'I told Mrs Stewart last night, Theresa, that the work is too much for you and that she must get a girl to help you.'

'It's quite all right, sir.'

'We are none of us getting any younger.'

'No, sir.' Theresa looks at the old man who is shelving himself into his coat.

'Perhaps you know of some young woman who would be suitable. I know that you probably think that I am stepping into my wife's province by discussing this matter with you but I am anxious to get this settled as soon as possible. I'll take it up again with Mrs Stewart when I get home tonight.'

'But, sir, with Richard off to London and Cedric gone for several years, we could shut off some of the house.'

'I wish the girls' rooms to be left as they are.'

'I understand, sir.'

CHAPTER TWENTY-EIGHT

SINCE THIS, AS I HAVE SAID, is not exactly the story of Cedric per se, I've no intention of detailing his passage through the next few years. Sufficient to say that in his immoral manner he managed to scoop up what dividends he could in the moribund British Empire. Odd jobs here and there, administrative bits and pieces, the odd lecture tour kept body and soul together. His knowledge of far eastern culture was quite extensive by this time and, using this to add to his eye, he accumulated a vast number of trophies. During a quick excursion into southern China just before the revolution finalised matters he managed to garner a number of priceless vases of the Ming and Sung dynasties. I have already, in my various books, written of these years and if you care to go to the British Museum you could see one or two pieces that I actually donated to the country.

But of his soul? His heart? There are sordid snapshots in sleazy hotel bedrooms that flash to mind. I could nearly list them cinematographically: not all, of course, because by their very repetition they'd bore the reader stiff.

Cedric sits on the edge of the bed. The lady – Rosalie, French, married to an English businessman – is leaning over her stockinged legs. A light-sleeved chiffon wrap, moss-green, slides around her narrow hips. 'If I could talk French to you I might understand you better,' she says. 'You never say anything real. I like men who say pretty things. You don't even tell me your occupation.'

'Buying!' Cedric is busy with his shoelaces which have knotted themselves irremediably. Finally he pulls off the shoe which flies into the air missing Rosalie by a fraction.

'Buying? What? Drugs? Opium?'

'Is that what your husband's in? Opium?'

Cedric wants to tell her that the British were the cause of the Opium Wars but feels this might complicate or slow down matters.

'I never enquire in my husband's – how shall I say? – deals.'

'Just as well.' Cedric has now released himself from his nether clothing and climbs in between two grey sheets. There is a broken fan in the corner of the room, the sight of which makes the temperature seem even more unbearable than it is.

The lovely Rosalie – for she is lovely in that sturdy French way – shakes off her wrap and slides naked into the bed beside him. There's a frenzied moment of sticky bodies being thrust too close together because of the hollow in the middle of the mattress and Cedric tries unsuccessfully to organise a position of gentle caressing without smothering the woman entirely.

'You tell me you have two sons. You must be very versatile,' she says when she has got her breath. 'And your wife, she is in America?'

'I don't consider myself married any more. I don't think I ever did. My marriage lasted about three weeks.'

'Are they twins?'

'Are what twins?'

'Your sons.'

'Oh, no. What I meant was the excitement. And that was actually before I got married. So I am a horrible man. See.'

She would have liked something more from me. Her manner was teasing, pleasant. We could throw banalities across the hotel foyer in front of her husband. But the complication of children and husband made me extra careful with my emotions. Sufficient to say that I missed her when they finally left on one of their business journeys.

There was a Malaysian woman. Quite beautiful, especially her arms and hands. I think that one of the worst ageing processes with which we northerners are afflicted is the disfiguration of hands. Some end up shiny like the backs of frogs, others mottled like figs; joints swell arthritically, lumps form. But easterners seem to keep that lovely oily flesh unblemished and she, although over forty, had the skin of a nineteen-year-old.

We hardly exchanged a word; she knew no English and my knowledge of Malaysian was of a practical nature.

Another lady: English. The English ladies were always trying to drag Cedric into bed. They were excited by this Irishman with his shock of black hair and his lack of attachments. They re-created Cedric, you might say. And he fell quite easily into this role of playboy, adapting an amiable shell like an outfit bought from a high quality tailor and paid for by a bouncing cheque. They had passed on long before they got the note saying, refer to drawer.

It is not easy to shut yourself off from these people, so I suppose that Cedric was not entirely to blame for his sexual proclivities. And he wouldn't have thought much about it had he not always had those emotional reservations that are the bane of all Irish men and women who've escaped from a dry Protestant web.

Sometimes he extricates himself from the interminable drinking sessions of gossip and fake sentiment and retires to his own room to make notes, write letters or a series of belated postcards to his parents. Usually: 'My stay here has been prolonged. Give my love to Theresa.' He also writes regularly to his wife, sending the monthly money. The letter friendly, distant. He looks forward to news of the children.

His letters to Theresa herself? Scrawls and scratches, unposted, lie among his papers. Her letters, too, when they reach him are scattered everywhere. They are like petals to him, from a flower that won't die. Yet the content is anything but frail. Her comments are earthy, pithy, unshy. About Richard's wife: 'Everyone's dream of the perfect Irish colleen with a mind like a hammer. Two daughters have come in quick succession. She carries her pregnancies like a sack of spuds stuck out front and poor Richard is half dead from embarrassment each time he brings her home. She keeps patting her stomach with a sideways eye on her spouse. I wonder how many more they'll have.'

Too bare, yet they fill that hungry space between midnight and dawn that eats into the mind, when the thoughts are so loud you can actually hear them. He'd chuckle over the memory of the old house as though it were beside him, or ready to take flight from Killiney and settle outside his hotel window. He'd talk then to Theresa about the dead sisters; he would learn things about Maria, about how she'd hide behind the box hedge with her drawing pad, the terrier drooling at her feet. How she'd taken to chain-smoking, lighting each cigarette from the end of the other; 'She'd go through sixty Craven A a day.' How she'd grown a little moustache and how she used to rub it with pumice-stone. And all the time he'd have glimpses of her galloping wildly across the scattered stones of Calary, the white-gloved hand and the leather crop, the tail of her bay mare winding like an aeroplane propeller, a habit she once told him it had. And of Jess, the one abiding memory of when he had brought her an Angora bed jacket and she'd thrown it angrily on the floor. 'Only something to wear in bed?' Two darts of anger in each unyielding eye. And how he had lamely picked it up and replaced it in its wrappings of tissue paper. How insensitive could he have been?

★

There are voices and strange smells. Smells like cinnamon only more penetrating. 'Natives of my mind,' he keeps repeating to himself. Breathing is difficult. It's as if he's trapped in a bog hole between two shelves of turf. With a supreme effort he opens his eyes. There seem to be people swimming in a bronze mist. The sun is trying to break in between the shutters. The noise of a fan reminds him of when a herd of cattle broke into the kitchen garden at home and their hooves tore the vegetables into tiny shreds. He can hear the rushing of their feet while being vainly chased by the cowherd. What were cattle doing in Killiney hill that day? he wants to ask these bronzed strangers. An aged Malaysian woman looms out of the mist. Her flat face is furrowed with hundreds of circular lines like a child's drawing of a football to which he has added eyes, nose and mouth. And there is another sound this time: it's like Father's old Morris Minor growling up the hill. But that was sold for scrap long ago. Gradually the present begins to take form. Two English-women are standing each side of his bed. They are singularly like each other. Sisters? Mother and daughter? Their skin is yellower than that of the Malaysian whose face is as brown as tea. One of them – the one with lipstick on – is holding out a glass of water. He wants to say, 'Don't throw,' but can't form the words.

She doesn't throw it but says in a voice that sounds as if it's been scorched by desert winds, 'The doctor'll be here soon. Stay quiet. You're going to be all right.'

They or, rather, the doctor insists on emetics and his throat chokes on old undigested food. He rolls about and moans. In the hospital to which he is carted there is a mixture of bad British organisation and wonderful Malaysian hospitality. He's treated like a king by the Malaysians and like a subversive by the nicotine-breathing English doctor. Englishmen – but then of course he's Irish and therefore either mad or bad – in his book don't go in for suicide. He is brusque, unclean and downright rough with his hands.

Back in his hotel, weak, recovered, ashamed, he writes:

Dear Theresa,

The Mrs Worthingtons and Mrs Whittakers are driving me round the bend. I'm scarcely on Christian name terms with them before I tire of them. I watch their daughters salaciously. I followed one to her bedroom door, a startled pretty face, and when she turned she said, 'Oh you're Mummy and Daddy's friend aren't you?' She reminded me of Jess before she got so very ill. Do you think I'm becoming a dirty old man?

I tried to kill myself the day before yesterday (I think) and was brought round by two bewildered Gentlewomen. One wore lipstick and the other didn't. Do you think she was the shy one? She didn't speak.

He scrunches up the paper and starts again.

Dear Theresa,

Will you walk up to the white rock for me today and

He looks at the letter as though it will leave the table and blind him. He continues:

throw two round pebbles into the sea. One for yourself and one for me.

I should never have done what I did to you. I gave you hope. People like you and me shouldn't have hope. My father is the only hero. He stayed at home and worked. Every day. Punctual. Fair. Will you look after him for me? He never made the mistake of giving people hope.

CHAPTER TWENTY-NINE

A T LAST HE HAS FINISHED his second book. He has to return to England to get the plates copied. He boards the steamer with forty-two pieces of luggage. 'You'd need a team of elephants to get that stuff on board,' someone remarks. And he settles down to what he knows will be a long, boring journey. A motley crowd of semi-criminal dealers, businessmen and once again their wives or mistresses. None of the old conquistador British Tory diehards to be seen – they are all, he presumes, ensconced in their Surrey cocoons, mowing their lawns and exchanging plummy observations with their neighbours in the lunch-time pub. Where else in the world do you get such people? A unique animal, the ex-British raj. Six of one and half a dozen of the other. Preferable, however, are the fly-by-nights who, like himself, are out to scrape the barrel. Although in the end they talk about the same things, tell the same jokes, but with different accents.

He sometimes laughs at his youthful principles which seem to have no relationship with his present lifestyle. The old revolutionary – somewhat a maverick, it's true – is well hidden now under the helmet of the years.

Will you walk up to the white rock, my love, for me?

A woman settles herself beside him like a hen. She is all brown rugs and cackle. A Rhode Island red.

'You've been very stand-offish, Mr Stewart. All during the trip.'

'How did you know my name?'

'I peeped into the purser's list.'

'Very bold of you.' He tries to find a face under the mound of wool. She obligingly throws back her shawl and he sees, to his surprise, distinctly Irish features surrounded by thick wavy hair. The kind of dry hair that has no control over its destination and flies away from the head, doing nothing to enhance the face. Her face is boney, a bit crooked, bearing the weight of some forty years, and in fact he is reminded of the face of the tramp he and his wife encountered on Killiney beach all those years ago.

'You are from the midlands at a guess. Roscommon?'

'Not far wrong. Athlone town. A terrible place.'

'Really? I used to think it pretty: the river, the boats, Lough Ree. We went there once for a holiday. My father enjoyed fishing the lake.'

'I used to swim, I admit. But ... growing up there ... ' Her tone is mild yet emphatic. What has she been doing? Not a missionary. No. She doesn't look like a do-gooder. A pleasantly selfish woman, he thinks. For the first time since he's left home he feels faintly intrigued. A teacher? In an American school?

'I'm a tourist,' she states to his unasked question. 'My father owns a flour mill. I've been everywhere. All over South Africa. I spent the war years in Southern Rhodesia and longed for a civilised approach to human suffering. Down there they observe starvation and misery as though it were a third-rate music hall. I nearly married a white Rhodesian – out of sheer boredom. Thinking, if I had a child I'd have an excuse to live in such ease and comfort. Luckily my brain got unblocked in time. I returned. Europe. France, Italy, Germany – everything so sad, derelict. So I set off east. You?' she adds. 'You're educated. Not like the rest.'

'Well. I usually say I'm a dealer, a wheeler-dealer. I collate facts and collect artefacts. I'm a thief, actually.'

'You write?' she says, pulling her shawl over her head again. 'I tried keeping a diary for a while, but I gave it up. I hate reading travelogues. Unless it has something to do with sex.'

He sits up sharply. Is this the inevitable invitation? But the crooked nose is pointing straight out to sea. Perhaps this is a pity. Who knows?

'Where are you going next?'

'I think I'll buy a horse.' Now she laughs and he thinks of the pebbles on the beach being dragged back by the waves. 'Yes, and ride from Valparaíso to New York. Of course, it's been done before – or nearly. But it would pass a couple of years.'

So for once he has someone to talk to. This plain, lively woman who can't stop moving becomes his companion for the rest of the voyage.

CHAPTER THIRTY

EPISODES. YES.

Nearly four months later a journalist is telling Cedric he wants to do a profile on him. 'When are you going to Ireland?'

'I hadn't thought about it.'

'I'll be in Dublin myself shortly.' He has a tired face, this man, and Cedric feels a seam of pity for him. Imagine, at his age, having to scrape around for a few bob in this manner. 'I thought perhaps an interview there would be more appropriate.'

'Why?' Cedric asks, trying to keep from spilling his drink in the jostle and merriment. 'I don't live there.'

'But you refer so often to Irish culture in your books. You are a connoisseur of Celtic art, too, are you not, Mr Stewart?'

'I hardly consider myself Irish. I went to school here and university. The time I spent at home ... '

'Oh, come now, Mr Stewart. No need to be secretive.'

Cedric is looking at the back of a black woman whose dress is of a vivid red and who sparkles with spangles and bangles up her arms.

'Gew-gaws,' he mutters.

'What did you say?'

'Oh,' Cedric laughs loud. 'I was thinking of my father. Whenever he saw an overdressed lady he used to say she was covered in gew-gaws. Perhaps that sums it up for you?'

'I'm afraid I don't understand you, Mr Stewart.'

'Well, look on my book as a gew-gaw, an attachment to myself that serves to embolden me along further steps of perfidious thievery.'

'Ladies go in for, er, stealing, you mean?'

'If you like. Some do, I suppose. They are not immune from boredom any more than men. However, I don't want to discuss the sexual mores of the English race.'

'There you go, Mr Stewart. Admit you don't think yourself English!'

This could pall, Cedric thinks, but out of pity again he agrees to an interview later that month in Dublin. He has to go sooner or later; it might as well be sooner.

He is being crowded for a photograph with his publisher; an eminent art historian breathes towards him out of the crush. They exchange knowledgeable platitudes. No time or place for a beam of discovery to light on either of them. They shake hands agreeably and filter towards the drinks table, the most popular part of the hall.

A woman hails him from across the room, another from another corner. Is this what popularity means? he asks himself. For a moment he's sorry he didn't ask the boney Irish woman he met on the boat. There was a wry sort of humour on her that might have driven a wedge into this exotic gathering. He wonders what would happen if he suddenly dragged the tablecloth from under all the drinks and told them all to piss off. Nothing, he thinks ruefully; he'd just be branded as another eccentric Irishman.

He longs to go back to his Chelsea flat and relax over a large Scotch whisky while looking at his priceless toys. Priceless. He smiles secretly and sidles away from the latest hysterical onslaught.

CHAPTER THIRTY-ONE

THE PLANE IS LATE. AS USUAL. Heathrow is full of moribund people in pools of luggage waiting hopefully for the loudspeaker to illuminate their situation. But it is impossible to understand the garbled voice; every so often one gets up to look at the instructions on the tape, returns to his seat, orders another round.

He reads determinedly, sips a brandy, occasionally brushes the cigarette ash from his knee, thinks not for the first time that he should have taken the Liverpool boat, old reliable craft which dumps you near the Custom House along with the cattle and the holidaying emigrants; he never liked aeroplanes, is afraid of flying.

Pa is quite active, fusses when Cedric walks into the hall – the door was open, the night not yet fallen – and he holds his son's hand for a long time, the small watery eyes quivering with the smile that never quite reaches his mouth.

Mother is also in the hall, hovering: 'There you are, Cedric dear.' Her heavy clothes shaking over the square frame.

Cedric notices a small bald patch on her skull, the flesh blue-white, an uneven circle. Cedric had never known his mother as anything but grey-haired and Maria, although fair, almost golden as a girl, had hair of the same straggly quality. Jess, however, dark in comparison, had begun to grey already from the effects of the wasting disease. He wonders now whether his two sisters, had they lived, would have already begun to bald.

His father's pate, of course, is quite bare except for the even fringe running round the back of his neck – like a monk with a tonsure. His skull, however, isn't blue but nut-coloured and coarse.

'A good flight, I hope,' Father says.

'No, awful. The plane was four hours late at the take-off. I hope you haven't been waiting for me all day.'

Father has retired this year although he still insists on going into the office every other day. He imagines the dingy little place in Clare Street couldn't possibly function without him.

'I looked up the flights,' he says. 'There were several scheduled for today.'

Cedric is anxious to see Theresa, feeling the greetings will drag on forever. 'I'll take my traps up,' he says. 'You go back into the fire. I'll be down shortly.'

'I'm sure you've lots to tell us,' Mother says. The tone in which she usually addresses Cedric now drops over her voice like a muslin cloth. Cedric realises that it will be a sticky evening. All first evenings are sticky and drain one of invention or inventiveness before they even begin.

In his room he stares out at the darkening night. The open window throws up the noise of the sea; the wave-crashes at this distance sound like the regular breathing of some wild beast. The air, although fresh and pleasant, makes him some-what depressed.

He knows what the matter is but doesn't want to meet the trouble. He's afraid to see Theresa. How is it, he wonders, that someone who is always in your mind when you are far away, the tracings of her movements in your mind's eye, that when faced with the reality of reunion you are filled with an almost unbearable terror? He's afraid, mortally afraid, but he decides to make a bold fight to be at ease. No matter what.

She never comes to meet him in the hall. No, that is not

her practice. Always reminding him where her place is; that unique place in his heart but only when far from the rest of the family.

She enters the room and he's startled because he was just preparing himself to go down to the kitchen. He can feel her presence before he turns from the window. As though something soft had brushed his face. He shuts the window with a bang that shakes the room and stares.

There is a darkening round the skin of those elusive eyes, the whites still very white, and the smile that must come quickly – what was it he used to call it? a solution? – begins to play while he takes her in his arms. They hug so closely they can't kiss. What had he been afraid of? he wonders as he leads her back to the window and throws it open again.

'I was thinking the sea sounded like a distant jungle animal repeating a kind of wounded roar. Not a very original or even apt simile, would you say?'

'It's very mannish tonight,' she says.

'Ma's going bald. Do you think I should buy her a wig? They're all the rage in London now.'

'A little bonnet would suit her Victorian temperament.'

'She'd be furious!' he laughs. She is wearing tiny studs in her ears and they suddenly flare as she moves her head. It is quite dark now.

'Like the east. Night has fallen like a blanket just while I've been standing here.'

'You were here a while.'

'Was I? What kept you?'

'I was polishing the silver.'

It is so inadequate, this conversation, that they both burst out laughing. The laughter runs like little streams down their chests so that each can feel the other tremble.

'Why,' he says, 'it's wonderful.'

'Yes,' she answers and runs from the room.

★

Pa is very proud of the wine and talks a lot about it till Cedric begins to feel shades of guilt. What is he trying to tell him? That he has overspent? Richard has come to dinner and is sloshing around the sideboard being more of a hindrance than a help to Theresa.

Ma takes her plate in both hands when Theresa brings the vegetables, holding it up even after the plate is overfull.

Cedric feels himself fussing with his food. He has become a little fussy, has nervous habits with his hands which are inclined to move as though he were shaking off his gloves.

He hopes Theresa doesn't notice these signs of middle age. To his forty she is now fifty-three. Interrogatory, watchful, she is; waiting for me to realise how she has aged, he thinks. And I will not. I refuse.

And then the row.

Was it the first night? Or two or three nights later? Do you know, I can't remember. But it was during dinner.

Why do rows take place at dinner time? Joyce immortalised it, I know. Or is it something that always seemed to happen in my family?

Mother all-powerful, possibly ghoulish with her appetite, perhaps always wanted to consume us. Except Richard, of course.

But there were two rows!

One about James. And the other? Well, the other.

'James has written about money,' Mother says.

Cedric sits up, forgetting his egotistical reflections.

'He's broke?'

'Your father is very upset.'

'Never you, you old cow,' Cedric thinks.

'Well then,' Cedric says. 'I'm not without assets. How much would tide him over?'

Later, in the drawing room, he reads the letter.

The page glitters against the coals. Words jump out. His daughter has run away with an American tap-dancer (Cedric laughs, eyeing Mother for reaction). And she has to be helped out financially. Promises, promises. The I-love-you-more-than-your-moneys that have been said so many times in so many different ways.

His wife: ill; arteriosclerosis. And he minding her, watching her every day while her lover calls and waits downstairs. She hasn't a good word for him any more.

James! Cedric has always thought of him as the lucky one: the one who got away. But now he writes pathetically.

Mother, in profile, is a lump of grey granite. That Stewart nose, in youth attractive, dominates. Weathered, she could represent an Egyptian male god. Her disapproval of James's begging letter – of James himself – is writ large. She won't budge an inch for her youngest twin son.

The grey of the ink is like the watery image of trees on a clear canal day. His younger daughter has got some religious bug and has disappeared into a sect.

Poor James. Alone in a far country, crying for help, expecting a last minute forgiveness and a hundred pound note.

No. No. Cedric gets up and paces the carpet. Each step hazardous from the drifting flex to the standard lamp. He goes out and upstairs and unzips his briefcase. He writes a cheque for a hundred and fifty pounds, nearly his entire current bank balance, and writes.

Dear James,

I would send you more if I had it. But for the moment I'm stuck for cash. However, by the end of the month I'll be relatively comfortable and will be able to send you another hundred.

While my finances are in a happy state, I plan to send you four hundred a year from now on, a hundred at the beginning of every quarter.

I'm sorry things are so rough for you. What can I say?
Fate deals out the cards and it's up to us to trump them.

No no. Cedric scratches this sentence out. What does he
think he is? Some sort of High Priest?

I'll write more in detail later.
Your affectionate brother,
Cedric.

He places cheque and letter into an envelope and seals it.

In the drawing room Richard, who has been playing
billiards with Pa, has returned to the hearth. He engages his
mother in some lengthy anecdote. Pa is leaning over near the
lamp and reading *The Irish Times*. He holds the paper aslant
the light, his reading glasses half-way down his nose.

'I have sent some money to James, Mother,' Cedric
interrupts the flow. 'I'm going out now to post the letter.'

'Now?' Mother and younger son look up sharply.

'And why not?' He reaches for some stamps that are stuck
behind a photograph in the chimneypiece, licks them and
hammers them onto the envelope with the cushion of his
palm, a habit caught from his father.

In the kitchen Theresa is bent over the sink washing a final
saucepan.

'Come on,' he says. 'We are walking to the village to post
a letter.'

The drying of her hands is a ritual that he often remembers
when he is away. First she rubs one, the right one, from the
top of her wrist to the elbow, stretching and turning the
radius and descending the back of the arm. She repeats this
with the other arm. Then she pulls down each sleeve with
the same determination as would a boxer roll his up while
preparing for a fight. Finally she shakes out the towel and
throws it onto the rail over the range.

They climb the hill in silence. The avenue is dark as a cave. Bushes drip on either side but the rain has stopped and the air is light.

Cedric feels just now as if there are no days. Just time. Time which is now beyond his control. Previously time was infinite yet ordered, death something to be switched on or off. But now it looms a sudden force; a current which is dragging the whole family with it.

'Have you got thin?' he asks, trying to control a tremor in his voice by laughing shortly. They have emerged at the top of the avenue and the one street light casts a dismal green, making the bushes shine, the road in its circle a pool of water and Theresa's face a ghostly white triangle – a nun's face in its cowl – against the surrounding black. Or, with the lamplight sharp on her, perhaps more like a figure emerging from the shadows in a painting by one of the Dutch masters – every hair neat, the features in repose.

'Perhaps,' she says, laughs. 'I get tired of my own cooking. James's wife has a lover. That's why you're so depressed. You gave one of your family the benefit of the doubt and he's let you down.'

'Yes. Why do we imagine that if people give up the fight to "be" something they live happily ever after? Do you think he'll come home?'

'I hope not. You're sending him something?'

'I can spare it.' The recent rain throws a scent of pine trees at them as they descend the hill to Ballybrack; it reminds him unexpectedly of the spice markets in the east and he feels a sudden tug. To go back to that non-existence where this family and Theresa are just leaves folded and dried in the pages of a book.

'I should have visited him on my travels,' he ponders, 'but somehow I always felt he wanted his anonymity to be respected. Or left to our imagination. But apparently not. He writes home to beg. Make us all feel uncomfortable and Pa and Ma angry.'

'I don't think your father is angry.'

He will go back to London, the stuffy hours in the British Museum, the ridiculous parties, the transient love-making, and then another trip. To Africa?

Africa does not appeal to him. He has a finicky nature. Heavy masculine art is not really his to interpret.

'I'm becoming an old woman,' he says. 'Pa knows what's what. Work till you drop.'

'Work's your only man!' Theresa says. They both laugh.

'You're right. I'm taking things too seriously. But the tension at home gets under your nails, behind your ear-lobes.'

'Don't mope, not while you're here anyway. It's your job to cheer me up, don't forget. Have a chat with Richard tonight. He's not as precious as you think. His wife is nice.'

'Theresa!' Now it's his turn to laugh first and the laughter bounces down the hill in front of them like a beach ball.

'Nice!' He touches her arm for the first time. 'What is nice? Only the worst thing you can be. Strangers are nice if they don't shout at you. If they say please and thank you!'

And then suddenly he doesn't want to touch her but his hand lingers. He wants to be alone. But no, it isn't that! God! What is it! Is he entering another mad phase? When he'll give death another try?

She is wearing a light mac and the sound of its whisperings dominates the surroundings. He finds the noise irritating. They have swung into the village and the post-box stands sentinel before them. He pushes the letter into its inviting mouth.

'That's that,' he says. 'Shall we walk home the long way?'

Theresa worries about his mother; she may be needed at home. This makes Cedric more annoyed.

'For God's sake, woman, Richard's there. He's not

paralysed. And if she gets a stroke he'll revive her and prove once more how indispensible he is.'

'Shut up,' Theresa says, really hurt. They walk in silence on the road now, both mad with each other. But it's Cedric who breaks it first.

'Come to London with me?' He stops to stare at the dark shape beside him. There is a street lamp behind her now and he imagines his own face – a bit like his mother's – impassive, arrogant.

He has frightened her, he sees. She seems about to speak but suddenly shakes herself and walks on firmly.

'Well?' he says, quickening his stride.

'Thanks for asking me,' she says in low tones.

'But … ?'

'But.'

'Oh, you could leave them. We could train someone in to look after them … '

'When you are there, I am here. And that's the way it's always been. And always will be till one or other of us … '

'Don't die before me. I could stand anything but that.'

'You used to say you wouldn't mind my dying.'

'Only getting married,' he fills in. 'Yes, I remember.'

'And you were wrong.'

'You know, don't you? I was right then. But now death is blowing about everywhere. Do you think me indiscreet?'

'Indiscreet? Why?'

'Oh, I don't know.' He feels as clumsy as a schoolboy now; even the hollow sound of his shoes on the road seems overdone as though he were trying to prove his mental strength. Two young lovers, entwined, loom out of the darkness and pass them. He turns to look after them. They are logically in love, he thinks. That's logic. Two young daft creatures. In a year the single bed they share will be too narrow and one or other will be sexually bored.

'Do you love me?' he asks, still staring into the darkness left by the couple.

'I'm not answering that stupid question.'

'I suppose you must. Otherwise how could you be walking with me here?'

'Anyone might walk with anyone. It proves nothing only friendship. Enjoyment in each other's company. Can we change the subject?'

'What will we talk about then? My great plans?'

'That would be more soothing.'

'Where will I go next? With my itchy feet?'

'Why don't you do something dramatic? Like going overland to India. Then you could take in so many old civilisations in one go.'

'Really, Theresa, I'm not a teenager. I can forego my comforts to some extent.'

I think it began to rain then; it seemed that we'd gone the full circle. I do remember that we were cold and wet when we got back and I felt very miserable going back into the drawing room. Perhaps that's why I conducted myself so badly during the subsequent events. Who knows? It probably would have gone like it did no matter what my mood.

The drawing room is uniform with its shadows. The dirty tray with its spilled remnants of coffee sits on the tall-boy. Cedric lifts it and carries it down to the kitchen. Theresa has disappeared. He looks in the scullery and the pantry. A mouse scurries in a corner and the lazy Tomkins uncurls one paw and yawns, curls himself up again more tightly. He is in his accustomed place on the Aga. There is a refrigerator now where there used to be a meat safe and he remembers a moment of terror as a child when he saw a bat stretched across the wire front, dead; and fleas rising from it like dust.

So she eludes me, he thinks, while knowing that his dependence on her will bring them closer and closer.

The fire dominates the drawing room now. The 40-watt bulb on the standard lamp only lights up a small circle. Mother in her usual place sighs and smiles thinly on his return.

'I think your father wants a word with you.'

Cedric looks over to his father on his window seat. 'Yes?' he queries.

'I have recently made my will,' the old man says, 'and I have left the house to you provided you will live here.'

Cedric feels a cold ball gathering in his stomach.

'But Father … '

'You are my eldest son. I bought this place for you before you were born. I thought about it on my honeymoon in Dubrovnik. The bay there reminded me of Killiney.'

'Father, I can't promise this. You are asking too much.'

'How dare you talk to your father like that,' Mother growls.

'Mother,' Cedric lets the anger take over now. 'Don't you dictate to me when all your life you've avoided me, kept me at arm's length. And you too, Father. Have we ever had a real conversation? Why do you think I choose to live in England or at least use it as a base? Only to get away from the tension that you two generate in me. Anyway, I don't particularly like this house.'

'I cannot understand you. I've sacrificed everything … '

'Don't start that again. I was always grateful for your financial help when I was a student. Have I ever asked you for money since then?'

Cedric pulls up, thinking of James and his pathetic plea. The two subjects of his mother's hatred, or at least disregard.

'Father, please don't put that burden on me.'

He sees, as though beyond a veil, his father stiffening in the corner.

He shouts out, 'The place doesn't make a statement. It's all higgledy-piggledy. Dull. Not even ornate like some of the Killiney monstrosities.'

'How dare you! How dare you! I've put everything I've got into your comforts, your mother's comfort, the door always wide open for you and Richard … '

'Not James, Father. What about James? He's not welcomed here, is he?'

'I wouldn't turn him away. He's also my son.'

'About time you recognised that.'

'Very well. I'll speak no more about it.' His father is fuming. His kind offer – or what he imagined was a kind offer – shouted down most rudely by his eldest son. But Cedric can't apologise, having said some of the things that should have been said years ago. He looks furiously at his mother. She is brick-red, her face shining. Richard, strangely enough, has not opened his month once during this exchange.

Cedric storms out of the room and races up to Theresa's bedroom. Her head on the pillow, turned to one side, is still as death. He runs to her, thinking, God! it's happened. But on his approach she turns quietly, opens her eyes. He sags down on the bedclothes and bursts into tears.

CHAPTER THIRTY-TWO

SO THAT WAS THE LAST TIME I WAS HERE. I packed and left the following day. And it's been six years. Six years! What happened to Cedric during these last six years?

A longer hospitalisation this time. Heavy, nauseating drugs, the head full of wool. No visitors by request. No flowers on that mental coffin. The doors without handles for three weeks, then moved to an open ward. Then the walks in the gardens ... hours in the coffee shop. Beginning to read again. God! What stupidity. Will I never do it properly?

That: the recovery from it took nearly a whole year.

And the other five. No, I didn't travel. Just stayed in London. Finished, with immense effort, another book.

All that year, of course, I couldn't write home or communicate with Theresa. She wrote me twice but I couldn't answer. Then when I was out again I had nothing to say. I was empty. Beginning to work again was, yes, hell. Money had begun to dwindle but I kept on sending that ridiculous sum to James. He never thanked me. Presume he got it.

My rudeness to my father, I suppose, shattered me. I used to think: 'Leave the lot to Richard for all I care.' He should have the house, anyway, it's his due. He's been a 'son', which is more than I can say for myself. But now there he is downstairs – Father, I mean – hidden away behind his past, his present non-existent: myself, Richard, James, all the one. Only some spark in his memory lights on Maria, the only one with whom, perhaps, he had anything to share. But now that I've skirted through it all I feel I have to see the last chapter through. My father will die tonight, I suddenly realise.

I hurry down. I forgot to say that Theresa, tired of my whingeing, went back to the kitchen a few moments ago. This thought uppermost in my mind: there he is, in the chair I pushed him into, unable to breathe properly. Scoops of air sliding like gravel into his lungs. Mother is standing over him, the little elephant bell rolling over and over in her hand. The thin, tinny sound, she hopes, may bring Theresa or myself.

I pick him up and race back upstairs and put him on his bed. Under his shirt his brittle breastbone rises and falls like a criss-cross stick.

As I reach for the telephone – an extension of which sits at his bedside – I find myself trying to distinguish a strange calciferous smell which is somehow familiar. The wind outside orchestrates my confusion by banging against the wall and making the copper beech groan with each blast.

'Yes ... yes ... I'm Cedric. His son ... Yes ... My father. Thank you ... '

The doctor says he'll come right away.

All the while I'm watching Father. Willing the harsh breaths to ease so his going may be less painful. I try to say some gentle thing but things that were never said during a lifetime cannot be invented at the last moment.

'You have been a hero,' I whisper. A hero without stripes, without requited love, a hero who did no great deeds but who slogged away from nine to five all his life, making out deeds and wills, dry-as-dust communiqués with old Protestant ladies living in Glenageary or Greystones, transferring properties of clients who died intestate, all to put his two sons through university and send his dying daughter to Switzerland and keep the horses for Maria and see the last of the black sheep who lives penniless now in some distant land.

And because of his martyred life he became a tyrant and we all turned away from him. I watch the last breaths straining his body. From time to time I think he's about to say something but the effort is beyond him. Just before the end he opens his mouth and a black stream hurtles out, slides down his cheek on to the pillow. I close the jaw. He is dead.

But something strange is happening to me – has been happening to me these last few minutes. I am conscious of a feeling of tremendous pride, or perhaps satisfaction is a better word. I am walking up a steep hill; it is difficult because, although I'm leaning forward, every step I take throws the top of my body backwards. The hill seems to be winding between two high walls and every few yards there is a shallow step. I feel a fine breeze that cools me and lifts my hair occasionally. Suddenly I seem to have reached my destination because I walk through a door in the wall and meet my mother. She is young, not unattractive, dressed in a light powder blue costume made of tussore; she holds a parasol tilted backwards over herself and the table she is sitting at. In a rather surprised voice I say, 'You look like a Manet.' She doesn't reply but I sit down and together we watch two lizards darting over the terracotta walls. Minute particles of sand fall soundlessly as they scrape and cling with their tiny fists. 'They are like my thoughts,' I say.

After a while I call the waiter to pay for my slivovitz and Edith's citrus drink, but instead of the waiter a young plum-skinned girl runs out and takes my few coins. We do not speak but I hear as though from a distance the one word, 'dobre'.

'Good evening. I'm Doctor Fitzmaurice.' The restrained tones of the doctor bring me back to the present and I find myself staring at the wall behind my father's bed. It is lined by bookshelves and the books are strangely familiar. They are all mine. *The Count of Monte Cristo*, *Dr Dolittle*, the complete works of Dickens, Thackeray.

'Thank you for coming. I'm afraid it's too late.'

Thus spoke Zarathrusta, *The Sorrows of Young Werther*, *Alice in Wonderland* (Jess's favourite book) …

'No trouble. There would have been little I could have done.'

Three Penguin novels by Evelyn Waugh.

'I'll send a woman up to lay him out.'

Gray's Anatomy … that must be Richard's.

'Yes,' the doctor continues, 'he would have wanted you by his side at the end. He spoke often of you. He was very proud of you.

'He used to show me your postcards. I believe you are a very distinguished historian, Mr Stewart. You are a lucky man to have seen so much of the world.'

I remember a line of Whitman's:

> I am your voice – it was tied in you – in me it begins to
> talk and I feel a blanket of tiredness wrapped around me.

'Would you like to sit down?' I say, trying to make my tones audible; he has such a kind face, this man, with eyes soft and changing as bog water.

'No, no. I won't trouble you further. You'll have a lot to do. I think your mother … '

'Yes, I'll have to go down to her.'

'You look very tired, Mr Stewart.'

'Perhaps I slept for a moment or two. I'm not sure. Would you mind waiting a min … '

My body shakes as I try to rise; my foot has kicked against a box beneath the bed. It is my old school box overflowing with my marine collection. The names drift in and out of my mind: bladder-wrack, sea-mat, starfish, sponges, periwinkles, limpets ...

'Yes,' I say, my tones hoarse from my effort to control my limbs, 'it's just as I thought ... '

As the doctor's trim shoulders bob down the stairs in front of me he chatters away. 'These old houses, you know. A lot of damp ... of course, I like to see them remain in the same family ... It's terrible what's happening in the city now ... no feeling for the old ... '

'Yes ... I love this abominable place,' I say, feeling extremely puzzled.

Theresa waits for us at the foot of the stairs.

'Your father, Cedric?'

I take her hand in mine. I feel ashamed because I can do nothing to appease our plight. In a few days I shall be gone and her life will flutter away from her like feathers from a little bird. But together, at least, we stand at the moment.